Chaos or Crazy

Natalie R. Arnold

To Monica & Foster
Enjoy the Experience

Cover designed by : Samuel L. Dunson Jr.

Dedication

I dedicate this to the following people: Lashonda Fuller for telling me to finish my story and her brother, Jewtroe"Trey" Fuller III (Gone, but not forgotten) Grandmothers: Mrs. Minnie (Good Granny) Metcalfe and Mrs. Laura Arnold and to all my family and friends that supported my dream. God bless you all!

I have a special dedication to my college roommate and friend, Techemia McLeod that recently passed away last year (2015). Thank you for your laugher and spirit. I will remember you always!

Thank you, Mom

Table of Contents

Chaos "Or" Crazy

Chapter One

The Beginning

Driving down I- 65 South, I knew that this Homecoming would be different than any other. It has been ten years, since I left college and my life feels like it's just getting started. I have traveled down this highway for many years. Four of them have been for college. After college, the rest have been for reconnecting with my girlfriends, aka my sisters. Homecoming, while in college, was mainly the football game, the battle of the bands and a week of partying. Now, it's about showing everyone that you haven't lost it. Also, it includes two nights of partying, one football game you don't watch because you are tailgating the entire time, and a week to recover. Since I am seasoned (I don't like to say older), the crowd has gotten younger and crazier. Now, Homecoming to me is just about getting together with my sisters.

After years of going, I decided to take a break and not come to this fun, yet tiresome event. I'm not saying anything negative, but I am getting too seasoned for this. Year after year, everyone I know is not coming that much or not at all. Currently, I'm gaining more responsibilities at my job, so it's starting to become impossible to take off. Alabama Agricultural University has wonderful homecomings. The parties, battle of the bands, tailgate and etc… the list goes on and on. The only thing I can't stand is seeing people my age or older trying to get their freak on. They look crazy as hell, but I love to see people trying and succeeding at looking like a true ass at homecoming. On top of that, it seems that guys you haven't heard from in months come out of the woodwork.

I couldn't stand when guys would call me a week before homecoming to see if I'm coming. The sad thing is that they just want to have sex or get something sucked. I would ask them what happened to you calling me just to say hello. The guys would always get quiet because they knew that they just wanted a booty call. I would love to give them some, but I'm doing the celibacy thing, which is hard as hell. Well, I will just have to work through the pain. Anyway, I am ready to see my sisters and have some fun.

My girlfriends are experiencing different outcomes in their lives right now. Kim is getting married. Noel is living the luxury, single life. Monica, the married one, is still trying to act like she's back in school. As for myself, I have been freed from the bondage of marriage over four years ago. Although, I received a great education from AAU, I failed when it came to picking out a husband. My marriage failed due to my ex-husband's issue of keeping his penis in his pants. He never came to homecoming, but if he did, I could handle seeing the jackass. However, I am at the point in my life that I don't have time to entertain the devil. Anyway, my sisters will be arriving soon. All of the girls are well. I hope! Monica has been married for ten years, with three kids. Noel, is a successful business owner and Kim is about to marry the love of her life. I am happy for all of them because blessings are different for everyone. I knew my road was hard with overcoming a crazy, abusive relationship and having to start my life over again.

The blessing was that I didn't have kids with him, so I don't have to be bothered with his crazy ass. However, his mistress wasn't so lucky. I don't regret my life decisions, but I wish I would have listened to my gut.

Monica - Mom, Wife and Other Woman

Yes, I am so happy to get the hell out of this house for a weekend. I will be able to get my freak on. I am so tired of my husband and kids. I hope I will see Sean there, because I may let him take a ride on Monica's "Double-Decker Donkey" booty if he asks for some. My husband works and leaves me with the kids all day long. I used to work, but after having our first child, it was cheaper for me to stay home. I feel like I need to request time off just to get a break from the kids. I do love my children, but I need time with my husband. He wants to be the great provider, which he is, but it seems that I never get to see him. I remember when we were dating, it was all about me. Now, it's all about work. Yes, I am a selfish bitch, and I'm not ashamed to admit it. But, if others knew about this, they would think I was wrong for feeling the way I do. Yes, I should be grateful, since all I have to do is take care of the house and kids.

But, I have a degree just like him. Before all of this, I was a successful manager about to go places. I would travel domestic and abroad, just like Noel. I would remember meeting up with her in New York or Vegas, then, Jeff wanted to get married. Don't get me wrong, I love Jeff. He is a nice guy and all. Shoot, sex is not bad, once I taught him how to please me. But, he was like, "Why do we still need to use condoms since we are married now?" From that, I am the mother of three children. I know that once the youngest starts grade school, I am going to go back to work. Well, I know he seems to be so busy, however, he will not see me kissing on another man at homecoming. Yes, I am wrong for wanting to cheat on my husband. Shit, men do it all the time, without even shedding a tear. He has never cheated on me that I know of. I hope Sean shows up! I still love that man! He could do things to my body that took Jeff five years to finally get. He was my first boyfriend and everything else at AAU. He knew me like a book. I was both his freak and friend at the same time. I knew I wanted him to be my man, from the first time I saw him in the student center.

He was built and had smooth cocoa skin, a smile that could light up a room and a body that made everyone looks at him. He was perfect. We dated the entire time in college. He was everything to me. However, he always seemed like he was missing something. He would tell me that he was not whole. Distance was common between both of us. I thought I could make him whole, but he just disappeared after graduation and that's how I ended up with Jeff. Jeff was there when I needed him, but he seemed to have forgotten me in the process. He says that he loves me, but the love is gone. However, I will get my groove back at homecoming.

Noel- Independent and Impossible

I need some rest and it seems that homecoming is the only time I can get some rest and see my friends. I am so busy and tired of working day in and day out. I should be happy, but I am so lonely. Since college, I have had plans to be the biggest and the best. On this journey, I realized that having it all is great, but I wish I had someone to share it with. It's hard to find a good man, but I can find a jackass at every corner. It seems that men love women that kick their ass up and down the way.

When they finally meet a woman that is good, they don't know what the hell to do with me. I don't bring drama, children, diseases or issues to any of my relationships, but fear. Yes, I am afraid of love. I've never experienced it. I would not know love, if it bit me on the ass. There are probably some good men out here, but they are probably working as hard as me. Every day, I travel to different destinations because of my job. Although, I'm very successful, I only come home to a big house, a dog and my garden tub. I know that I could have been married or with someone millions of times, but I was too busy or I was scared of getting hurt. I have read hundreds of books on relationships, loving yourself and dating outside your race. Shoot, I have tried all of that and it still seems to blow up in my face. I even have flashbacks of rejections from college. Yes, I remember sitting in my marketing class and James came into the room. He was on the football team and was rough and nice at the same time. I did like him, but he told me that it could not work because he was no good. I never had a guy tell me that, but I guess I should be blessed that he was honest with me. I'd rather have an honest man than a liar. However, all men do it. I truly envy Monica's relationship.

She has three beautiful children and a husband that allows her to stay at home. She calls me a lot and complains about having to be at home. Shit, I would love to be able to be a stay at home mom. Yes, I make six figures and can buy anything I want, but I am alone. I do believe in God and I know He is with me. However, when I go home, it's just me. If I started to talk to myself, my neighbors would probably commit me. Well, I know that I am going to take a nap, before my plane lands in Alabama. Right now, I wish I could have a drink, but I better not.

Kim- Love at last?

I am finally getting married. God has blessed me with a wonderful man in my life and a good career. My life is wonderful. Planning for my wedding is driving me crazy, but I would not have it any other way. I am so happy that the girls are going to be in it. I hope Monica doesn't drink, because she is not a pretty drunk. My Larry is a man I thank God for every day. He loves God, himself and me. It's a wonderful feeling to be important to someone. Also, he is Cuban and loves some Kim, too!

I hit the jackpot with his sexy ass! It's funny how we met, because I came up to him at a seminar and asked him where the restroom was located. He looked at me and said, "Lady, I don't work here." I was so embarrassed to assume, but I had to go real bad. Anyway, he helped me find the restroom and even told me he would wait for me to make sure I got back to the seminar. We walked back and I took my seat. He walked up to the front of the room and introduced himself as the main speaker of the seminar. I felt like a true ass and sunk down in my seat. However, he kept smiling at me through the entire event. As I walked out, he asked me where he could get a cup of coffee and then asked me to join him. That was the best mistake I ever made in my life. I do hope something wonderful happens at homecoming. I thought I would never find love again, after what Donald did to me. It's like day and night with Donald and Larry. Donald would be so loving and wonderful one minute, and then treat me like shit in the next. I gave so much to him, but when I asked for the same in return, he would forget.

Sometimes, I wonder what would have happened, if I would have had his child. I could not believe that he told me a baby would mess up his life. What about mine? I can not change the past, but I know that my future is beautiful. Well, I am happy and Homecoming will be the icing on the cake for me.

Chapter Two

Checking IN!

Man, this city is growing bigger, since I was a student here. I know that I would like to get a nap in before the girls arrive at the hotel. As I walk towards the counter to check in, I saw a man that took my breath away and he was doing it again. Ethan Davidson! He was my friend the first two years of college. He was older than I was. I remember how we met. It was a warm September night and Kim and I were walking back from the Student Center. We heard someone calling out, "Excuse me, Miss?" and there was Ethan. He asked if I was an upperclassman, but I was only a freshman. "Maya, how are you?" asked Ethan. "I am fine," I replied. "I

16

have not seen you in a while," says Ethan. "I've been very busy," I told him. "I heard you got married, how is that?" asked Ethan.

"I have been divorced, for four years now," I said. "Oh, I am sorry to hear that," he said with the biggest grin on his face. "Are you with someone?" I asked. "No, but I have been busy with life and my son," said Ethan. With a proud grin on his face he said, "He is two and growing bigger every day." I thought to myself that it was wonderful. "How long has it been, Maya? It's been a while, since I last saw you. Are you staying in the hotel?" asked Ethan. I was wondering why he was asking these questions, but I said, "Yes." "I am waiting for the girls to arrive. I'm staying with some friends, but maybe we could have dinner or something before homecoming was over," I tried to say in a smooth and sexy way. "Well, I may have to take you up on that offer," he expressed. I'm thinking to myself that I really wanted to take a nap before the girls come and I wished he would hurry up with the flirting. "You take care, Ethan," I smiled to him. As he walked away, I was looking at his wide shoulders. I don't know why, but I love a guy with a big back.

It was nice to see some old faces. As I received my keys for my room, I saw a woman who had on some sharp shoes that I had wanted to purchase for the longest time. She was tall as hell, and built like a stallion. I straightened up a little, like my mother always told me to do. I put my chest out and stand up straight with your stomach held in. Since we were walking towards the elevators, I complimented her on the shoes. She was happy about the compliment then shouted out my name. I looked at her wondering how I knew her. Honestly, I am terrible with names and I am quick to say, "Hey girl or boy" to anyone. "Maya, Maya, It's me," the stranger said. I know I am not good with names, but her face wasn't coming up in my memory. "It's Sean, well, Sandra now," she yelled. Wow, Sean looks good as a woman. He looked good as a man. I was shocked, but all I could do was smile. "Maya, I have so much to tell you," she said. I kept smiling, but I was telling myself, Monica is going to be either happy or pissed. "When I was in college, I was well known and loved by everyone. However, I was not happy within myself.

18

I dated a lot of girls and even settled with Monica for three years in school, but I was lost," Sandra said. "After graduation, I left the country, trying to find out who I was. I realized that I was different and I embraced it. Now, I am a happier and healthier person." I am happy for Sean, but I knew in the back of my mind that Monica may not feel the same way. "Well Sandra, I am happy for you and maybe you can help me with some styles, because your outfit looks good," I said with a funny grin. "Maya, do you know if Monica is coming?" asked Sandra. I told her, "Yes." "Monica has never truly gotten over you, Sean," I told her. "I never got over her," said Sandra. I did wonder if Monica was willing to go from hot dogs to donut holes, but I felt that this was none of my business. Although, I was laughing my ass off, in my mind. "Sandra, Monica will be showing up soon, so I will contact you, if you want me to," I said. "No," said Sandra, "I want to surprise her." Well, I want to be there for that, I thought, but I answered, "Ok." Once I got off the elevator, I parted ways with Sandra and started to head toward my room. As I put my bags down to get my room key out, I heard another voice call out my name.

Yes, it was dumbass Donald. I could not stand this man. He was the type of man who acts like his stuff don't stink. He is a male ho or "Moho". Kim was so in love with him, but he seems to act like he couldn't care less about her. "Hey Donald, how are you?" I asked. "I am wonderful and know that I am blessed," Donald said surely. Donald always acts like he is the nicest guy in the world, and then turns around and knocks you up side your head. I remembered the nights when Kim was crying because he stood her up. Or maybe told her off, honestly, I don't remember, but whatever the asshole would do hurt my sister. He was so charming that he could get any girl he wanted, but Kim was the only one who would put up with his mess. "How is everything, Maya?" "Everything is great, Donald," I said waiting for his smart ass remark. "Well, I see that you are alone again, Maya," he stated in a joking way. "Well, Donald, that is by choice," I quickly said to him. He came back with, "Maya, I can see you like to be alone, maybe I could change that." I was ready to slap the hell out of him, but calmly said, "Donald, I am a Christian woman, so you need to leave, before I tell your ass off."

His mouth opened, acted surprised and stated, "Well Maya, I thought you were better, but I guess you are just like the other women." I rolled my eyes at him and expressed, "Well, Donald, I don't have time to entertain the devil, so go back from where you came from." After that, he started to walk away, but turned and said, "Well, tell Kim, her man is here." "Yes, I will tell her some jerk-off asked for her," I smirked. As the jackass continued to walk down the hall, all I could think about is how can I hide this from Kim and give him the middle finger, in the process. Finally, I was able to get into my room and lay down for a nap. I was happy that we had adjoining rooms. It reminded me of the old times, when we shared a dorm room with a common room in the middle. We had some good times. All of us were on different roads in our lives, but all of us wanted a chance for a wonderful future.

Chapter Three

Girlfriend Connection

"I am so happy to finally be in Alabama," said Kim. Everyone agreed to meet at the airport, since we are arriving on different flights. "Hey Noel!" said Kim. "Girl, I am ready to get the party started!" "Let me see that big diamond," said Noel. "Wow, I can not wait until the wedding," said Noel. "I am so happy," said Kim. "I will say one thing, you better have a moist cake," said Noel. "People don't care about how beautiful things are at the wedding. It's the cake that will get you in trouble," laughed Noel. "You don't want a dry cake, do you?" "Girl, you stop that, you know my cake will be the best and most moist cake ever. It will have pudding in it," laughed Kim, then she said, "Well, I am just happy to see you and know you are doing it, lady!" Noel just stood there with a blank look on her face.

"Noel, what is wrong?" said Kim. "I am so tired," said Noel, almost coming to tears. "I work day in and out and I am so alone. I know that a man will not complete me, but I am ready to share my life with someone. Even God said that you can not live by bread alone," she said, looking frustrated. "Noel, I truly believe that love comes when you least expect it," said Kim. "I was always looking for love with Donald, and then we broke up. I did not understand how a man could say he loves you and crap on you in the next turn. When I was alone, I had to truly focus on God and myself to heal. When I finally got my game in order, Larry came into my life. The amazing thing was I did not even look for him, but he was sure looking at me. Once I opened my heart up, he came in and that is all I can say about that. Noel, keep faith and allow your heart to be open to anything," said Kim hugging Noel. "Now, we have to get to the hotel and wake Maya up, because I know she is taking a nap," giggled Kim. Maya loved some naps.

"Knock, Knock, Maya!! Get up, girl," said Monica. "Girl, I was sleeping well," I yawned. "How are you, girlfriend," she said, hugging me. "I'm good," I replied. Monica asked, "Are you ready to get your freak on, Maya?" I laughed and said, "I guess, I don't know about getting freaky, because it's been so long since I did get freak on. I have more dry seasons than rainy ones." We laughed. "I could get lukewarm and drip half way," I joked to Monica. "Girl, you are silly," said Monica. "Now, I want to do it like BBD," said Monica. I looked at her crazy and said, "Monica, what are you talking about?" "I want to bump and grind," Monica said, dancing in the room. I actually forgot what BBD stood for, but I did not want to mess up Monica's good time. "Monica, can you stop giving me sexual song titles and tell me what you are talking about," I stated with a concerned look on my face. "I want to have sex with Sean," said Monica. My eyes popped out of my head and I said, "What!?" "If Sean comes to homecoming, I want to have sex with him," said Monica as she licked her lips.

I started to giggle, because I knew that Sean was not the same guy from college. "Maya, what is so funny," wondered Monica. "Nothing, but I know one thing, I doubt you will be doing anything this weekend without the help of a bullet," I said with the straightest face, without laughing my ass off. "Anyway, I want to feel like a woman, Maya," said Monica. "Monica, what are you talking about? Is there something wrong with your marriage?" I asked. "Maya, I just feel like Jeff doesn't want me and that he may be cheating on me." "Well Monica, I hope you don't cheat to have one up on him," I told her. I know one thing about a man who cheats. My ex-husband would blame me for everything or think I'm cheating on him, if anyone gets friendly with me. I remember one time, my ex got mad that I was going to church. The saddest thing was I did not know that he was cheating on me. "Monica, you doing wrong will not justify his actions," I told her. "If you want to get your groove back, get a vibrator because its disease free and if you don't want to be bothered, take out the batteries," I said. "Maya, you are silly," laughed Monica. "Monica, I had a reason to leave my ex. If you and Jeff can work it out, do it.

I sometimes wished I did not have to go through my divorce, because it's hard out here. You don't know if someone is lying or telling the truth. It's like playing guess the card and hope you don't get the joker," I explained. Monica just rolled her eyes and said, "Anyway, I just hope Sean shows up soon, it would be wonderful to see him and get down to business." "Well, whatever happens, you will get what you deserve," I whispered. I knew that was wrong, but Monica is the type of woman that would need to be shown something to change her mind. "Monica and Maya, how are you doing, girlfriends?" yelled out Kim and Noel. The gang was all together. It's funny, because I remember how all of us met. It was our freshmen year at AAU. I was washing my clothes, one Saturday morning and watching TV in the main hall. I remember Monica came down and sat in the room. We were both watching TV and began to chat with each other. What really made us cool was someone came by the dorm and said that the football team was having open practices down the way and we decided to go in our PJ's. We had the hair rags on, house shoes and everything else you could wear to bed.

We did not care and it was cool to have someone who was laid back. We walked all the way to a football practice on the other side of campus with what we had on, and then went to breakfast. I met Noel during the freshmen candlelight celebration and Kim through Noel. All of us were different, but it makes our friendship special. When we come back to homecoming, a lot of people cannot believe that we're still together. Although all of us have separate lives, homecoming is the glue that connects us. It's the foundation of our friendship and sisterhood that keeps us coming back year after year. We cried, laughed, and even sat in the ER at the hospital together. We have always been there for one another. Homecoming is important, but I'm scared to tell my sisters that I truly want to take a break from doing this.

"I got all your bridesmaid's gowns for the wedding," say Kim. "Girl, I want to meet some of Larry's friends," said Noel. "Kim is so lucky. She got herself a sexy Cuban Man!" I yelled. Kim was blushing. I knew Larry was good to her in many ways.

"Yes, madam, I want to get my groove on and eat some good cake." I laughed. Kim asked, "What is it about the cake? Are you guys for real? Then she said, "Larry and I decided to have the ceremony in Cuban and English. I have been learning the language in order to say my vows to him. I think it's wonderful, even though I will not have the slightest clue of what you will be saying." "Kim, you are half Chinese. You barely get that right," giggled Monica. We all started to laugh. After Monica stopped laughing, she responded, "Well, don't worry, we will all be there." We heard, Knock, Knock on the door. "I will get it," said Kim. As she opened the door, it was Donald. Kim gasped and said, "Donald, how are you?" "Missing you, baby," grinned Donald. Now, I knew it was going to be on because Noel cannot stand Donald. It's like pizza to a person that has frequent heartburn. There was going to be a lot of pain coming up. "Hey, you can leave now," said Noel with the look of someone who was going to get their feelings hurt. "Oh, Noel, you look wonderful," said Donald with a devilish smile. "Donald, Kim is getting married and you are not the one," giggled Noel.

Donald looked at Kim with sheepish eyes and asked, "Is this true, Kim? Are you getting married? I thought it would be us." I am thinking to myself, this fool is crazy as hell. He treated Kim so badly and always placed his life and dreams first. Kim was always placed second, third or until he felt like being bothered with her. I remember when Kim got real sick with food poisoning. We took her to the hospital and stayed with her all night long. We called Donald, because she was calling for him and we tried to get him, but I guess he was busy. However, I found out that Cindy Henderson was the one that made him busy that night. I knew that my ex was more of an asshole, but it's not about me right now. "Donald", said Monica, "I know you have someone in the wings. You always seem to have that." "Well, Monica, I am a changed man," stated Donald. I knew the only thing Donald would change was his mind and drawers. Men don't change, unless they truly want to, and I just don't see Donald doing that. "I won't keep you ladies. I will see you later, Kim." said Donald. I shouted out loud, "Bye, ASSHOLE!! "Look, Donald could be a changed man," said Kim.

All of us simultaneously looked at Kim, as if she had lost her mind. I said, "Kim, do not go there and mess up what you have with Larry. Larry was a God-send. If he could be cloned, I would want someone like him." The saddest thing is it seems that when you have been married, you can see a good man quicker, because you have been with an awful one. It's hard out here. However, I encouraged her by saying, "We are going to be at your wedding Kim. We want you to be happy." I know Kim, and in the back of her head, she is debating both men with her head and heart. Kim is like all women, including myself. We want to know if we made the right choice, even when it's the wrong choice that gives us a large amount of proof. I'm thankful that I was awakened by my experience with a crazy-ass man. Because now, I don't have time and can weed him out quicker than grey hair on a black Lab. Kim leaving Donald was a chance for a better life. Larry finding Kim was an opportunity for them to build a friendship and love. I think of them as a door opening and closing, at the same or different times in life.

I pray that I will have a door opening up for me soon, with a fine man on the other side. Noel asked, "Well, what's on tonight's agenda?" Kim has been the party planner since college. She knew where all the hot events were and if we should go to them or not. "The Lighthouse is having a "Back in the day" jam and we should go there," said Kim. I was excited except when I heard, "Back in the day." I know I am 32, but I can't stand to hear "Remember back in the day" starting a conversation because it just pisses me off. However, Monica is good at bringing the attention back on her. "I know I want one thing to happen, I want to see Sean," said Monica. She smiled that same old grin when she was about to get it on with Sean. I remember back in the day, when we would all be in the dorm room listening to Mary J. & Monica. My room would fill up with the scents from our body sprays that we purchased at B&BW. The scent would turn guys on! I remembered one time a guy told me that I smelled like potpourri. I just smiled and took it as a compliment. Although, he sounded country as hell, it was nice of him. We knew when Sean and Monica got together; she would come back looking as if she was attacked, but in a good way. However, I knew she wouldn't be getting attacked, especially by Sean this weekend or beyond. I started to laugh. Monica turned to me puzzled and asked, "Maya, what are you giggling about?" I told her that I was just thinking about the times we would get ready to go to the club back in the day. Damn! I just said the phrase I don't like to hear. Well, we didn't have a car, but we always found a ride to get there. I was the only one who stayed sober, because of the fear of Monica getting into a fight. That girl could throw down some drinks. One time, in the dorm, we got some beers and she would put a hole in the bottom and pop the top. It was so amazing! So, I usually had to wait till I got back to enjoy some spirits.

The Lighthouse was the place to be, when I was in college. When I entered college in the mid-90, the music at that time was a movement. We had Biggie Smalls, Tupac, the Fugees, Uncle Luke, and Bone Thugs. The list would go on and on and the club played it all. It was cool that the club was holding the old school party. (In which, I am not happy that I am now considered old school).

However, the music was good and you could at least understand what the people were talking about. "Girls, we are going to have fun tonight," said Monica. Monica was the wild child of the bunch. All of us had our code names. Monica was "Wild Child", Kim was "Sweet Thang", Noel was "Baddest B. or BB", and "Smoov" was my name because I could smoothly tell a man off. However, I wasn't that angry anymore. Each of us had the power and we exercised it with the men and in other ways that will be revealed later. Anyway, all of us would come together and leave together when we went out. Now, when the men came into play, we would still leave together, until we got back to the dorms and leave from there. "I cannot wait to see Sean," moaned Monica. "I am going to get my freak on with him." I thought the only thing that would be freaky is Sean, aka Sandra, going to the Ladies Room with us. I want to tell Monica so bad about Sean, but I think maybe she should see it for herself. "Monica, what is going on?" asked Kim, "Why are you about to mess up you marriage over Sean?" "Look, Kim, I don't want to hear it," said Monica, rolling her eyes.

Monica continued saying, "Donald came in here and looked past all of us to you. He wants you and he doesn't give a flying fuck about you and your engagement." Kim told Monica, "Don't worry about me tonight. You cover your own ass." Man, I hate that Monica started drinking early, because she cannot hold anything. I remember when we were with our guy friends and all of us were about to go to the Mountain, the guys made some "swamp juice" which was made of all types of liqueur and Kool-aid for color. She drank one cup full and Shrimp had to pick her up and carry her up to the room, because she was messed up. To this day, she said it was the cold medicine she took earlier that day. Well, we will see how Monica will act tonight. I'm afraid for Sean/Sandra, because if Monica gets crazy, she may try to hurt her. However, may the best woman win! Just the thought of the whole situation makes me wonder how everything is going to play out tonight. Monica sipped her drink, licked her lips and said "I want Sean, and I know he will want me!" Monica trying to shake her ass in the mirror just looking like a hot mess. I looked at her and thought, yes, tonight is going to be something.

Chapter Four

To-Nite is ALRIGHT?

Everyone is starting to get ready to go out. All of us would get ready in different ways when we were back in school. Noel would have planned the entire night. She would make sure that we would have the ultimate night of fun. Kim would talk to Donald prior to going out and we would have to make her feel better, because Donald would make her feel guilty for going out. He is a true asshole. Monica would get her drink on. I remember one time she got so drunk that we had to do an intervention to get her to stop. She still drinks, but she handles it better than in the past. Myself, I would turn up the radio, because music was my mojo. The sad thing was I would always be the first one ready out of all the girls. Experiencing life and being out of college for a while, things are somewhat different. I still get ready faster than anyone.

Monica gets buzzed off of coolers. Noel finally goes with the flow and

Kim does not call Donald. We finally got ready to leave and everyone was

looking good. As we walked down the hallway, some young boys started

to holler at us. One of them licked his lips. The only thing that it did was

put moisture back on his cracked lips. Another has a gold tooth and had

the nerve to say, "You ladies look good, but you are too old for me." I

turned around and told him, "That's ok because you look too broke to

me." We all laughed. Noel commented, "Do you know what checking and

saving is? You need to be checking yourself, because someone may need

to be saving your ass from all of us." We laughed again, even harder. As

we got on the elevator, I saw Sandra coming out of her room, but she

wasn't alone. Before the door closed, I waved to her and her company. As

the door closed, Noel said, "That's James with some lady." I could not

believe that James was with Sandra. My mind was going crazy. I wanted

to say something so bad, but I had to respect what Sandra asked of me.

Monica stared at her and asked me if I knew her. I just smiled and told her

that we all do. "How?" asked Monica.

I told her that we were linked by someone whose name started with the letter S. I'm laughing inside, because I was ready for Monica to meet Ms. Sandra, her long lost lover. Also, I was shocked to know that James is Sandra's man. Damn, this night is going to be crazy! After getting off the elevator, I saw Ethan. He was looking good, as heaven. There's something about a clean man that makes me smile on both lips. "Good evening ladies," said Ethan. Noel said, "Hello Ethan, how are you doing?" I looked over to Noel and she looked hungry as if she hasn't eaten in a while. I'm thinking to myself that I love my girl, but this meal is mine. "Maya, you look beautiful as always," said Ethan. I thought to myself, yes, you look so good that I would like to see you somewhere with water running over your body! However, I just told him, "Thank you." Ethan gestured to a guy to come over to us and said, "Ladies, I want you to meet John, one of my Frat brothers." Noel's eyes jumped out of her head. "I got to go to the ladies room," said Noel before she quickly dashed away. I thought she was running a sprint, because I saw a smoke trail behind her. "Excuse me," I told everyone and ran to the ladies room after her.

"I can't believe it. John is here," said Noel. I asked, "Who is John?" She turned around to me and said, "He was the man that I fell in love with and he asked me to marry him. However, I turned him down for a position in New York." Wow, I thought and said, "Maybe this could be a good time to talk to him." "No," said Noel. "When I left him, I did not talk to him. He called and called, but I was so ashamed and afraid," she said with her head down. I put my hand on her shoulder and said, "Noel, we all make mistakes, but maybe this time will allow you the chance to correct it." "You are right, Maya," said Noel. "I am going to go out there and have a good time. If John approaches me, we can talk about it." As we walked out of the restroom, I saw John walking toward us. "Noel, I just wanted to say that it's nice to see you," said John. "You are looking good yourself, John," said Noel. John asked, "Are you still in New York or traveling around the world?" "No, said Noel, I am settled in Maryland and happy. Are you with someone?" He smiled and said, "I'm with someone special." "Oh," said Noel, who stomach was now at her feet. "We are all going to the Lighthouse. Why don't we finish talking there," said John. "That would be nice," said Noel. After looking at everyone, I knew this night

was just the beginning to a lot of crazy situations. After looking at John, I

realized that Noel had good taste, but bad timing. Once we arrived at the

club, there was a line forming outside the door and not like in the old days

where everyone would be slammed against each other. The funny thing

was a lot of the jocks would be able to walk into the club. The girls would

yell out that there were too many guys going into the club without an

equal amount of girls to match. Someone would always shout out,

"Something was wrong with that!" Majority of the time, the jocks would

also be the bouncers, so they would always get the other teammates in all

the time. After walking in the door, I realized that the first thing I wanted

to do is find a seat because my feet would hurt like hell. Now, I learned

that the older you get, comfort trumps fashion.

As we entered the club, I saw so many faces I knew, but didn't have any

idea of their names. Half the night, I was saying, "Hey, girl or guy," to

everyone. Honestly, I was never good with names, but great with faces.

Kim and I were enjoying ourselves at the table, while Noel and Monica were making their rounds at the bar. I saw Sandra and James approaching our table. James looked like an ice cream dream walking with her. "Kim!" Kim looked at me crazy and asks Sandra, "Do I know you?" Sandra said, "Yes, Angel cake." Kim looks again and jumps out of her chair and asks, "Sean, is that you?" "Yes, the one and only," she said. They hugged and Kim was looking at Sean like he was amazing, but was tripping out at the same time. "I love your shoes," said Kim. Sandra looked at me and asks, "Maya, have you told Monica about me?" I wanted to say yes, but I knew Sean would know I was lying, because I would struggle with words. "I think it would be best for you to tell her, but not now," I told Sandra. Sandra grabbed James's hand and said, "I'm sorry that I have not introduced my friend." As the guy came closer, I realized who he was. It was James Jones. That was the guy that Noel liked in school. Well, now I understand why James said he wasn't good for her. Man, all of this is happening and Monica and Noel are nowhere to be seen. "Ladies, I'll be heading back to the hotel to get some rest. Come on baby JJ," giggled

Sandra, as she walked away. Well, although this situation is different, I'm happy for both of them. Everyone deserves to have love in their life. Monica appeared out of the blue and asked, "Who was that couple that walked away?" Kim's eyes were popping out of her head and she started to laugh out of control. Kim was speechless, but she was laughing like she would when we would watch Def Comedy Jams back in the dorm. Noel said, "One of them looked familiar?" Kim grinned and said, "It was James Jones." "That was James? He looked so good," said Noel, as she was fixing her hair. Noel looked at me and asks, "Maya, why didn't you stop him?" I had to remain calm for Sandra's sake. I said, "James has a woman. Her name is Sandra, and she was pretty." Monica was starting to look frustrated, because her sexual release, Sean, wasn't at the club. "I don't see Sean anywhere," she snapped. Kim and I looked at each other and grinned. "Guess what Monica, Sean is here," said Kim. I hit Kim's arm under the table so hard that the table moved a little. "I must try to see why he didn't want me after college," Monica dramatically expressed, trying to fix her makeup. Why does it seem like I'm always the bearer of bad news or any news to the girls? However, this time I was not getting involved. I was going to stay out of the picture. "Excuse me ladies, I would like to dance with Kim," asked Donald. Everyone looked at him like he had crawled out of the gutter. "That's fine, Donald," said Kim. As they walked to the floor, I dipped my finger into my red wine and flicked it on the back of his nice cream colored shirt. It's funny, because he felt something, but probably mistook it as water from the mist machine. "Kimberly, you know you smell and look wonderful," said Donald in a smooth voice. "Donald, we had our run, but life moves on and so did I," said Kim. "Well, what if I told you that when you left me, I missed you so much." Kim said, "That's funny because it took you two years before you even contacted me after I left. Donald, I will always love you, but I am getting married." Donald quickly asked, "Well, if your man loves you, does he make you feel good the way I use too? I knew what made you happy, baby. You were the best thing to me." "However, I wasn't the only woman that you made happy," snapped Kim. She quickly stepped back from him and said, "I am sorry, but I have to go." "I am going to get you back, baby," stated Donald. As

Kim walked away, Donald turned to the mirror and saw the red stain on his shirt and got pissed. He thought someone on the floor did it, but I knew who did. I was laughing my ass off looking at the entire situation. He started questioning people with wine in their hands. As the night went on, I realized that I talked to more people that knew me and I did not have one clue about them. "So, are you calling this a night, when you get back to the hotel," said Ethan, as he slowly crept up behind me. "Well, I would not mind going to the bar at the hotel and talking with someone, if you get my drift," I said. Ethan said, "Well, I will meet you there in about an hour." As he walked away, I had another flashback on how I met Ethan. It was a beautiful September night and the girls and I were walking to the Greasy Spoon on Campus. All I knew was some guy with other guys following him called me over. I stopped because I was interested to see who it was. Ethan had on a baseball cap over his eyes and big baggy clothes since it was the 90's and big clothing was in. "Hey, what's your name?" he asked. "Maya," I said. He asked if I was a senior, but I said no. I asked him, "What's your name?" "My name is Ethan and I'm a senior," he said. I was scared, because I've never been with an older man. So, over time, we became friends. I thought that something would come from it, but nothing did. Sorry, for the repeat, I just love telling that story. Ethan was always a respectable gentlemen and there for me in college. It's weird, but he always made himself available to me. I was very young minded at that time. Kim tipped me on my hand and said, "Maya, look who's here?" I looked up and it was my ex with one of his girlfriends' or baby mama. I wasn't surprised to see him here with whomever, but she should know that if he cheated on me, he was going to cheat on her. "Hello, Maya," my ex grinned. "Hello," I said. Then, I got up and walked away. I don't have time to entertain monkeys, so I left. As we walked to the car, Monica and Noel were looking upset because they did not leave with any phone numbers. Kim looked at her engagement ring and smiled, while I thought about the night not ending until I get to talk with Ethan. This night may have ended on a crazy note, but we still have one more day and night to get there. Lord, please be with me!

Chapter Five

Night Cap + Drama = Hot Mess!!

As I drove back to the hotel with the girls, Monica kept complaining about why she didn't see Sean. I wanted so bad to tell her, but in her condition it probably wasn't the best time. "Maya, did you think I was stupid for dating Donald," said Kim. "No," I said. "I was wrong for marrying my ex. However, it taught me a lot about myself. You have a chance to have happiness with Larry. You need to cherish that opportunity." "Maya, you know that you have the same chance as me, too," said Kim. "Sometimes, I feel like I don't, but I know deep down, I would like to experience a good relationship," I told Kim. I know that only God would know who that man would be, because all the men I dated in the past can just stay there. As we arrived at the hotel, I saw Sandra and

James in the parking lot kissing and going at it. "Hey! That is James," shouted Noel. "Who is the woman he is ripping up? Do you think she went to college with us?" asked Monica. "Maybe," said Kim. Only Kim and I knew it was Sean, but it was not our place to tell Monica anything. "We need to go by and say something," laughed Monica. I thought to myself that we should leave them alone and let them do their thing. "Nonsense, we have to be nice and friendly," joked Monica. I knew when Monica said that she was just being nosy. As we got out the car, Monica shouted out that they need a room. Sandra shouted back saying, "We already have one, we're just starting the foreplay here." Kim and I were trying our best to get Noel and Monica up in the room. As Monica walked closer, she told them, "You both are acting like how my man, Sean and I would, before getting the party going back in the day." Sandra stops kissing James and says, "Go on, I would like to know." I was thinking loud, "O, Hell!" "Well, Sean and I would start in the parking lot, and then go straight to the dorm. We would make sounds that only translators could understand," Monica started to laugh like crazy after the comment. "O, my," said Sandra. She cleared her throat and asks, "Was one of them, Daddy slam it like a Jordan dunk?" Monica's eyes widened and said, "Yes! He would jump on the bed with his pen…" Then, Noel looked at Sandra and gasped for air, "Sean, is that you?" Monica looked at us and said "This is a woman, not a man." She turned and saw Kim's and my face with a confirming look like, yes, this is the Jordan's slam dunker. Monica ran up to Sandra and looked like someone stole her joy. "What!?" Monica was mad, confused and drunk at the same time. She yelled, "I wanted to have sex with you! How are we going to do it, now? Where is your penis? You got rid of a very good penis!" "Let me explain," said Sandra. "Explain what? You left me as a man and came back as a woman! I was about to compliment you on your outfit and shoes! Not now, buddy! Your outfit looks like shit," screamed Monica. All of us just stood there trying to look calm. Monica looked down for a moment and tries to say in a calm voice, "Your shoes look nice as hell, so I will give you that. I wanted to sleep with you!! I needed some love from a man, not girl time!!!!" As the yelling went on and on, I decided to leave because I had a night cap with

Ethan. Before I reached the door, Monica ran crying and looking like she was going to be sick. Noel murmured behind her that maybe that was the reason why James didn't like her. However, I knew James tasted both sides of the field. Everyone in college knew that. As for Kim, she told everyone who could hear her that she was so happy to be getting married soon. Hey, I cannot blame her. Anyway, I walked into the bar and saw Ethan and John sitting there waiting for a drink. I walked in and Ethan got up and pulled out the chair for me. I sat down and told him about what just happened. We laughed, but I knew Monica was hurt, because she wanted Sean. In a way, I'm happy that it happened the way it did. Monica was about to endanger her marriage. "Maya, you still look the same as you did in college, but better," said Ethan. My head was so big! I just smiled and said, "Thank you." He took a sip of his drink and asked, "So, how has life been treating you?" I said, "Well, I cannot complain. It has its good and bad, but I am blessed." "Yes, I can understand that," said Ethan. Ethan stared at me and said, "Well, Maya, It's good to see you. I'm still sorry that your marriage ended." I smiled, "Thank you, but I have been divorced for a while now." "I'm just glad that you're doing well," said Ethan with the biggest grin on his face. I was wondering why he was asking about my divorce again? Maybe he was just making sure I was really divorced. "Thank you, but I am fine," I expressed. Hell, I was happy, but the MF was here acting like a jackass. However, when you are that way, it's hard to fake it. Ethan licked his lips and said, "Well, you look great. Maya, I wanted to ask you something?" I was wondering what he wanted to know. I knew I was not going to do anything, but don't think I didn't want something to happen. I would be happy just for a kiss. I yearned for more, but I wanted more in my life than sex. He asked, "Do you think things would have been different, if we would have been more than friends?" I was thinking to myself, Hell, I don't know. I stated, "Honestly, I don't know. I know I respected you and didn't want to mess up what we had." I thought to myself, we can be friends tomorrow and I will let him grab my booty right now. I told him, "Maybe time will tell a different tale." We smiled at each other. I wanted to sit down there forever and not go back up to the room. However, I knew very soon that I would have to go to bed.

Chaos "Or" Crazy

"Maya, I'm tailgating tomorrow with some of my friends. You and the girls are more than welcome to join us," said Ethan with a smile on his face. I smiled back and said, "Well, I will take you up on the offer. I guess I better be heading up stairs and see about Monica and Noel." "Have a good evening, Maya," he said, as he got up and hugged me. It's been a long time, since I had a man hug me, but I will not put a lot in one hug. He smelled so good, that my nostrils were having an orgasm. As I walked out of the bar, I saw Sandra. She was not happy about the fact that Monica now knows about Sean. I guess she wished for a different response. "Maya, I am so upset and I need to talk with Monica," she aired out to me. I just said, "Sandra, I don't think it would be good right now because Monica is drunk and Noel is upset." Sandra was confused and asked, "Why are they upset?" I had to remember that Sandra has just become a woman. I told Sandra the truth about Monica wanting to see Sean's penis. "It's not you, but you are lacking the one thing Monica wanted from you. You are now just one of the girls. Monica was horny and wanted to have sex with you then, not you now," I tried to explain. Sandra said," Lord

50

knows I can go to church and give all the information about men, but I just wanted to see about Monica first." I didn't understand what she meant by that comment, but I said, "Sandra, let's wait until tomorrow, after she sobers up and her mind is right." Man, I wanted to go back to the bar and get a drink after everything that is happening right now. "You're right, Maya," said Sandra, with tears in her eyes. It felt like college all over again. This was the same crap that happened when Sean and Monica had a fight and I had to calm the storm. The only thing about this time is they won't be having sex to resolve it. Maybe, they could go shopping together after all this mess blows over. As I was walking towards my room, I saw Donald creeping out of one of the rooms with lipstick kisses covering his face. "Maya, can you tell Kim that I will be out at tailgating waiting for her tomorrow?" said Donald. I turned and said, "Ok, I will tell her that you are full of shit!" After he walked away, I gave him the finger like I always did in college. As I approached the room, I hear Monica and Noel still complaining. I opened the door and saw Monica pacing back and forth. Noel was on the bed shaking her head. Kim was smart. She was in the other room asleep, because she could sleep through anything. Monica stood in a daze and said, "Maya, Sean is a woman!! I cannot sleep with a woman!" "Well, now we know that you could, but there will be more licking than screwing," I said, jokingly. "I cannot believe that James is gay! That's why he never paid any attention to me." I wanted to tell Noel that we knew something was different the night of the Halloween party at Dunn Hall. It was an awesome party and everyone was dressed up. I was a witch, Monica was a Swedish maid, Noel was a nun and Kim was a policeman. I remember showing up to the party and Sean and James came as the Indian and Leather guy from the singing group, The Village People. To make a long story short, they tried to request "In the Navy" and "YMCA" all night long." Monica asked, "Maya, how long did you know about this?" "Honestly, I found out when I checked in this afternoon. I told her that I loved her shoes and I was surprised as much as you. I think Sandra is happy and that's all that matters." Monica wasn't happy, because she could not get some. I knew how that felt because I don't even remember the last time that I got some. What am I thinking? She's married and that's a blessing. I did a fake yawn and said, "Well, ladies, I am going to bed. I'll see you in the morning for breakfast." As I left the room, I was laughing my ass off, because of what their faces looked like. After closing the door, I whispered, "Kim, are you asleep?" "No, but I was playing, because I did not want to talk about what happened," said Kim. She turned around towards me and asks, "Maya, do you think Donald changed?" I wanted to say no, due to seeing him coming out of someone's room earlier. "Kim, I think you should believe in what you feel about the situation," I told her. I don't like to give advice because people never listen, but I will give my opinion. Kim whined, "I felt that Donald still cared about me, but he hurt me so bad." "Well, Kim," I replied, "I think that if you want to go through hell again, you can get back with him or enjoy the happiness you have with Larry. It's up to you, my dear. All I knew was I had to go to bed soon, because tomorrow is another day. After what happened tonight, I need all the rest I could get."

Chapter Six

Good Morning :} Hot Mess with a cup of coffee

Monica, knocking like crazy on the door, yelled, "Get up, girls! We have to get some breakfast!" Yes, Monica may have been mad last night, but she would never miss breakfast. Even in college, she could be out all night long and still get us up for breakfast. Noel didn't want to go, but we told her something crazy to get her up. We always threw on anything and headed to the restaurant downstairs in the hotel. I saw a lot of people from school. I saw Ethan and John, which made Noel kind of happy. We saw Sandra and James, which made Monica's eyes roll to the back of her head. In addition to this, Donald gave Kim a smile which just made all of us sick. "Ladies, May I have your order?" asked the waitress. We always get the breakfast bar and as we headed there, each of us was met by someone. "Maya, you look good in the morning," said Ethan. I grinned and said,

"You don't look bad yourself." My mind was wondering so wildly! I wanted him so badly to touch every part of my body. Hey, I need love like anyone else. Ethan asked, "So, we got a tent and we will be set up near the stadium. Will you come by?" I told him, "Yes, I will make a way to see you." "Good, I want to see you, too," said Ethan. After that, I knew in my mind I was going to have a good day, regardless of whatever else will happen today. "Monica, I need to talk with you," said Sandra. Monica gasped and said, "I don't have anything to say to you except, why?" Sandra moved in closer and said, "Please don't make a scene about this. I am happy and I want you to be happy for me, too." Monica shouted, "Well, I AM NOT! I wanted to do you and I needed it from you!" Everyone in the restaurant turned to look at them and all I could do was shake my head. "Monica, you are getting too loud," whispered Sandra. Monica stormed out of the restaurant and Sandra ran after her. Donald bumped into Kim and she smiled a little. "Kim, my Be Be!" It was Larry. He came and surprised Kim and she was. "Hey, baby! I thought you were home," smiled Kim. "No, I had a business meeting here, and I remembered you told me about your homecoming. Maya told me the hotel you were staying at and here I am." Donald looks pissed and I looked at him with the most devilish smile while eating my bacon. I looked at him and thought to myself, "Yes Jackass", the game stops here. "Noel," said John, "I wanted to know if we can talk later." "Yes, but, I may be busy," replied Noel. John reached for her hand and said, "Noel, I just want to talk with you. It would be nice if you could make time for this." As I sat down and looked at everything that was going on, I was so happy that I didn't have anything messy going on. Yes, I knew my ex was here. However, I wasn't going to let anything get between all this drama and craziness that was currently going on.

"Monica, we have to talk now," demanded Sandra. Monica looked at her in a questionable way and asked, "I don't understand why you did this?" Sandra asks, "You're mad because I'm a woman?" Monica started to tear up and said, "NO! You left me, Sean. I loved you, but after graduation you disappeared. You didn't tell me where you were and I never got to tell you how much I loved you." Monica was trying to talk with tears streaming from her eyes. "Monica, I wasn't happy with myself," said Sandra. "You did nothing wrong. I was messed up and when I left college, I left the country and started to learn something about myself. I was living a lie for a long time. I have always loved you, but I knew you wouldn't understand what I was going through." Monica asks, "Did you trust me?" "Yes," said Sandra, while touching her face, "I trusted you would be you, so I had to leave." The relationship we built was only on sex and rebounds. The marriage you have with Jeff is built on something more than what we had. Jeff loves you. However, you were selfish. It was about what you wanted than what you needed." Monica rolled her eyes because of Sandra's words. "Honey, love is not selfish and you were willing to mess up your marriage for some homecoming booty?" questioned Sandra. "No, I just wanted some love from Sean," said Monica. Sandra started to walk away and she turned back and said, "Well, if I was Sean, I wouldn't give you anything." Monica just stood in the hallway, feeling like a true ass.

After finishing a wonderful breakfast, I started to head back to the room to get a little more sleep before the game. I saw Sandra walk away and Monica just standing there with tears in her eyes. As I walked up to her, she looked like she wanted to ask me a question. We got into the elevator and Monica turned around to me with a sad look and asks, "Maya am I selfish?" Well, I thought, yes, however, I had to softly tell her, "Well, Monica, you wanted to sleep with Sean," I said. "Are you not happy in your marriage?" "Jeff just doesn't give me what I need," said Monica. Then, I asked her, "Do you tell him how you feel? Men don't know what we think. We have to tell them letter by letter. If they don't listen, then that's their problem. I know Jeff would listen to you." Monica continued wiping the tears from her eyes and said, "He does, but it's not the same." I'm thinking to myself, what is this not the same crap. I explained, "Dear, you and Jeff have been married for ten years and you have three kids. Things don't stay the same. You and Jeff are not the same, but you have to tell him how you feel, because how would you feel if he did this to you. Has he done this to you?" "No, Maya," said Monica, "He loves me and he has never done anything wrong." "Monica, you better wake up before you make that man go into the arms of another woman," I snapped at her. "Sometimes, we help our men into the arms or beds of other women." "Is that what happened with your ex?" questioned Monica. "No, he was just an asshole and male whore in the beginning. I was scared to leave him because of all the crap he took me through," I said. "My ex was never satisfied. I could do everything right and he would still want to be with another woman. Not all men are bad or good, they are just men." As we walked back to the room, Sandra came running up to us. She stood in front of her and said, "Monica, I have to say one more thing to you, now!" Sandra grabbed Monica's hand and led her back to her room. I stood there for a moment and wondered how did I get myself into this mess? I headed back into my room and jumped back into bed.

Monica sat in the chair of Sandra's room and they stared at each other as if this was their first time ever meeting. Sandra sat on the bed with tears running down her face. Monica nods, but is still lost for words.

Monica played in her mind the times of Sean holding her and making love to each other. She could not believe this was happening. "Monica, I am happy, said Sandra. "I am happy in my skin and with who I am. For years, I battled with this decision, but when I look in the mirror as Sandra, I know I made the right choice." Monica yelled, "Sean, why didn't you love me? I waited for you after graduation. You disappeared and came back like this? You are an asshole for not loving me." Sandra walked over to where she was seated and gave her a tissue. She looked at her and said, "Monica, I loved you too much! That's why I left. I was confused and you didn't deserve a fucked-up man. You are beautiful and intelligent. You could have had any man you wanted." Monica whispered, "I wanted you, Sean!" Monica got off the bed and looked quickly at the mirror and stated, "Damn, I wanted to make love to you. I came to homecoming wanting to feel you, smell you and taste you." Sandra said, "Monica, you are married and have children. We would have never done it. I love and respect you too much to mess up what you have. Why are you willing to mess up your life over one night?" Monica sat back down on the bed with her head down, saying, "I'm not happy with my marriage and family." I guess she thought she was going to get some kind of sympathy from Sandra, but she was terribly wrong. "No, you are not happy with yourself!" yelled Sandra. Monica jumped off the bed and screamed, "How dare you tell me that!" "Happiness is something you first have to have with yourself. No man, child or sexy-ass woman like me can make you happy," Sandra explained to her. "YOU DON'T KNOW ME!" said Monica, with tears streaming down her face. Sandra softly said, "I know you, Monica. I know you are strong and hard-headed, but you're not a cheater or whore. You are overwhelmed with life, choices and opportunities. Monica, I wanted to marry you. I had a ring in my pocket at graduation, but when I saw you walking across the stage and smiling your wonderful smile, I realized that I wasn't worthy of you. I would have been living a lie and hurting the one person I loved the most. So, I disappeared, knowing that I could not come back the way I was." Monica has a sick look on her face and asks, "Do you like men? Were you with any guys when we were together?" "No," said Sandra, drawing close to Monica and sitting her down on the bed. "I was faithful to only you. I loved you. I still do. Currently, I have dated both sexes. However, this is my first serious relationship. I feel safe with James. When I told James about my transformation, he supported me every step of the way. I knew about James in college. I didn't judge him. We remain cool to this day, because I treated him like a person." "Well, Sean, I don't understand why, but I am happy for you," said Monica. Sandra hugged her and said lovingly, "Sweetie, you are blessed to have a family that loves you. Do what you were going to do with me to your husband. Show him the way you showed me. I remember you loved it nice and slow." "Yes, I do," grinned Monica. "You will always be my friend and we could go shopping. I could teach you how to dress," said Monica. "Sorry, you are the student and I am the teacher this time around," laughed Sandra.

Chapter Seven

Reflections

As I was lying in the bed, I thought about all things that are happening to me. I wasn't happy or sad, but feeling some kind of way. The divorce took me from hell and back. However, a man or woman should never stay with a person that doesn't give a damn about your sanity. I can honestly say that I was not in love with my ex. I tolerated him, because after everything he took me through, I felt no other men would want me. I had to get out, because I loved and respected myself too much to be taking the crap he gave me. The sad thing is that he still thinks he did nothing wrong. Well, I will stay hopeful for love, but for now, it's all about me. "Maya!!!" yelled Kim as she came crashing into the room. "I don't know what to do! I love Larry, but Donald can still get to me," she said. I was facing the wall and rolling my eyes, because I knew that I was not going to get a nap in before the game. I knew this would happen. Every time, Kim gets confused over Donald's dumb-ass. I understand what she is going through, but she's got to make up her mind. I slowly turned around and looked at her. I was trying to think about everything before I said it, so it wouldn't sound rude or thoughtless. "Kim," I said, "You have a choice. You can have someone that loves you or the same crap that kicked you in the ass constantly." Kim just stared at me and said, "I guess I couldn't take the same situation again. Maya, Donald still loves me. Don't you see it?" "Honey," I said, "I see the same man pulling the same crap, year after year. If he loved you, why doesn't he call you the remainder of the year? If he loved you, why doesn't he respect you moving on and that now, you have a good man? If he loved you, why did he do the meanest shit to you? Kim, Donald can't love you, because he doesn't know what love is, unless it's for himself." Kim's eye started tearing up so bad from my comment. I knew she was scared. Hell, I am scared too. It's hard to get back out in the world after a failed marriage or a bad relationship. People are now crazier and quick to say or do anything to get what they want. "Kim, I know you are scared, but I know Larry truly loves you. I can see it. He makes you a better person. Donald didn't do that at all. Remember the time you were together and you stayed at his apartment and he went to the club with his friends. I saw him grinding on some girl, while you were at his apartment waiting for him to get back. He doesn't deserve you. You deserve what you're worth and that is the best," I said to her. While Kim was wiping the tears from her eyes, her question was, "Maya, what if Larry hurts me?" I understood how she felt. The last thing you want to do is get involved with a man to go through the same mess, but that's the chance you take with love. "Honey, no man is perfect, but you don't need a man to complete you. You got to have all your stuff together before that one man comes into your life. After my divorce, I discovered that I love myself to the point that I don't need a man. I want a man in my life to share the love I already have to give. One day, I know it will happen, but until then, I will keep improving myself. Shit, look at me now! I'm fine as hell, but humble too. Kim, please don't let go of something new for the comfort of old crap," I smiled. All of a sudden, there was a knock at the door.

I was wondering who that could be. I looked out the peephole and saw Larry. Kim started to jump around like a crazy person, trying to get herself together. "Hey Maya," he said, as I opened the door. Larry walked into the room with a proud look on his face. Plus, he smells so good. It's been so long since I smelled a man. "Baby, I wanted you to spend time with your friends, but I was in town and it would've been rude of me to not see my baby girl," he said, smiling from ear to ear. Kim jumped into his arms and kissed him so deeply that tears were falling down her cheeks. I told them to go into the other room, so they could have privacy. Plus, I didn't want to see any more of their foreplay.

"Larry, I'm so happy to see you," Kim softly spoke into Larry's ear. "What's wrong baby," as Larry gently touched his hand to her cheek. Kim asks Larry, "Baby, do I make you happy?" "Kim, you made me happy the first day we met. You make me a better person. The love I have for you is special and I want to show you how much I appreciate you by making you my wife," said Larry, kissing her hand. Tears started to stream down her face. "I love you too, Larry," she said, as she smiled. "I just get scared sometimes."

He grabbed her waist and pulled her closer to him. "Baby," he said, while looking into her eyes, "We have each other and God. We can work out anything that may come our way." As they were about to kiss again, the door flew open. It was Noel looking for Monica. "Hey, Kim and Larry," Noel said, as she looks desperately around the room, "Have you seen Monica?" "No," said Kim, "Not since breakfast." Noel ran into my room and jumps on the bed and asks, "Maya, have you seen Monica? I am getting worried. I'm looking for her." She was acting like a crazy person. I was thinking that I need to start charging people for all the time they come and bother me. Man, it takes me back to the dorm, when everyone loved to jump on my bed, while I was taking a nap. I was the guru that everyone came to. Man, I did not know anything back then. I would just let them talk, while I listened. I am a great listener. Honestly, most of the time, I was thinking about something else during the entire conversation. But, I learned how to pick out the key words so they wouldn't think I was not following them. Shit, men do it all the time. "Noel, Monica is fine," I said. "I just received a text from her that she's with Sandra." Noel looked like a big weight was taken off her shoulders. "OK, as long as she is ok," said Noel. As Noel jumped off my bed, the door opened and it was Monica. Shoot, I jumped up because I wanted to hear what happened, too. Monica came in the room and sat on the bed. Noel and I just looked at her waiting to hear what took place. She stared at us and said, "It's weird, but nice to know I have a friend." "I guess so," said Noel and I looking at each other. I was wondering what the heck she was talking about. "Sandra is a good person. Sean was a nice guy, but he makes up well as a nice woman too," Monica murmured. I agreed with her, but she was acting kind of out of it. "Maya, I'm not happy," she said. "No shit, Sherlock," I whispered under my breath, but Noel heard it and hit my arm. All I could hear is the money coming in if I was a psychologist. I went into the wrong field! Noel felt bad to see Monica like this, but there was nothing she could do. I wanted the atmosphere to become light, so I tried to change the conversation. "I never thought Sean would totally become a woman," said Kim, coming to the room and sitting on the bed with Monica. Damn! I guess so much for changing the conversation.

She said, "I never told anyone, but I had an idea a while back. At night, I would go walking on the campus to clear my thoughts. I was around the gym when I saw Sean. However, I saw him with a guy from the football team. The guy was massaging his shoulder, and I did not think about it. Then, I saw the guy starting to kiss Sean on the neck. I was shocked as hell. However, Sean turned around and pushed the guy off and ran away. I quickly walked away because I did not want him to see me. I never told you this Monica, because I felt it was not my place." My eyes got so big, and so did Monica's. To me it was like, Ok, it makes sense now. Monica couldn't say anything. Her mouth was frozen. All I could do was look around the room, because I was stumped myself. "I was about to have an affair with Sean, but that won't be happening now." I looked at her as if she was crazy at first, but now I kind of felt somewhat sad for her. I finally snapped out of it and said, "Monica, can you hear yourself?" She dropped on the bed like someone placed a 50 pound weight on her shoulders. I continued to say, "Why, Monica? Why are you trying to mess up your marriage? Why don't you tell Jeff how you feel?" She screamed, "Maya, it's not that easy! Jeff doesn't make me feel like he used to, like I'm important." "It's not all about you, Boo," I snapped. "Honey, let me tell you something. Just tell him how you feel. It's not worth being selfish and messing up a good marriage over what could have just been a weekend fling." Monica jumped off the bed and shouted, "It's the little stuff, Maya! Jeff works long hours and when he comes home, he wants time to himself. I come around him with sexy lingerie and he goes to sleep!" I was playing the tiniest violin over Monica's situation. I said, "Monica, you don't even have to work. He is allowing you to be home with the kids and gives you the option to work or not. I'm sorry, but if I had that, I would do whatever to make that man smile." She rolled her eyes and yelled, "Maya, I want him to spend time with me!" I pointed out to her, "Monica, make time for him. Run a bath, massage him in the nude, do something! Do you yell at him?" Monica stared with sad eyes and said, "Sometimes, he doesn't listen." I rolled my eyes and said, "Shit, I would not listen to someone

70

yelling or nagging at me either. Do you ever thank him for what he is doing?" She answered, "No, but he should be doing it anyway." That was the first time I realized that Monica drove Sean away. I sighed and explained, "Monica, you have a man that is willing to provide for you and the kids. Be blessed, because a lot of women are just praying for a man that has a job and would treat them right. You need to set up some sex time. It only takes 10 minutes or less to give him some booty and build up your relationship with Jeff. My mother told me that you will not always get what you want in a man. However, if you get what you need then be happy with that. Talk to Jeff, he will listen to you." "Maya, you think you know so much," she retorted. I stared straight at her and said, "I know one thing, Monica. I am not happy being alone. I hate that I gave my heart to a man that didn't give a shit about me. My ex had an affair and produced a child with another woman. In addition to the abuse and infidelity, he still acted like he didn't do anything wrong. Jeff is a good man and you should not mess it up over selfish reasons. You have to realize that you have a man that stands beside you and loves you and the children. I am still praying and hoping for a chance like that. I thank God that I didn't have any children with my ex because my child would not have a good role model. My child deserves a father that will show him or her love, support and how a man should treat me as his wife and mother to them. I pray that my ex gets his life in order for his child. However, after that, God can worry about him. He made his decision about what he wanted and I hope he gets everything he asks for." "Maya, I never thought about that," Monica said, apologetically. "Yes, Monica, you are not thinking. You are selfish as hell. You got everything and still not happy. Honey, I want you to understand that you've got to be happy with yourself and love that man. If you don't, there will be a woman trying to see if she can love your husband better," I confirmed. "O my God, I don't want that to happen," yelled Monica. "Well, all I can say when you get home, love on that man and tell him thank you or something. My mom always said you can get more flies with honey, than with piss," I advised. "Well, I will do that, since it's been a while since we had sex," she confessed. "What! How long has it been?" I asked. "8 months," she replied. I yelled, "Monica, are you crazy? You can have sex available 24/7! Are you both sick?" Monica said, "No, I got mad at him and did not want to give him anything." I told her, "Monica, you better screw the hell out of him when you get home." She gasped, "Maya!" I said, "Monica, I am serious. I have not had sex for over two years and that is by choice. Married sex and single sex is so different. They both start off awful, but with married sex, you get better with time. Single sex, you have numerous partners that are all awful. Plus, they think it's great, but there's no emotion in it. Shoot, the guys don't even know how to satisfy you the way you want. So, I decided to focus on getting myself together." "I feel you, Maya," said Noel, "I just need God." I gave Noel a crazy look and said, "Noel, I love God too, but I want a man. I need some love and love making. However, I can be miserable by myself. I don't need help. Plus, John made your eyes come out of your head. Why didn't you marry John?" She answered, "I loved John so much, but I loved my career. I traveled and made good money. When he asked me to marry him, I got scared. So, I stopped returning his calls." "Wow, Noel," I exclaimed, "So are you going to finally tell John why you didn't marry him? I think he deserves to know the truth." "Maya, I am a successful woman," she said. "Yes, a successful and lonely woman," I told her. She came back at me by saying, "Maya, how can you say anything?" "I know I'm not where I want to be, because I had to start my life over. I got my MBA now, and I'm trying to make my life work. I hate where I am, but I'm not where I was. I would be lying to you if I didn't. Noel, you had love and when John came into the bar, he looked at you. Tell him the truth. If you can make it work, do it. However, if you screwed it up take it as a learning experience."

Chapter Eight

Second Chance?

Noel was a successful woman. I couldn't understand why she let John go. He is a fine and talented chef, but did not make the money that Noel was bringing in. I remembered when Noel would tell me about John surprising her with moonlight picnics and edible sex. I never heard of it, but she was happy when she called me afterwards. Well, John is here at homecoming with Ethan. It's kind of cool and funny at the same time. But, I wonder if they would ever get back together. "Maya," Noel said, interrupting my thoughts, "John is now a successful chef at a restaurant in New York. I saw him on a cooking channel show judging a competition. I am a fool. I let a good man go. Do you think he would take me back?" In my head, I was thinking, Hell no. You messed up and that ship has sailed.

However, I told her, "It's on him." It's hard to know if a man has moved on or still wants to make amends. I'm not a doctor of love, but I don't know too many men going back, unless they truly love that woman. Noel loved John. I saw it in her eyes. They must have been happy. Love is a funny thing. Well, I knew I needed to get out of the room for a moment. Everyone's situation was getting to me and I needed a break. As I left the room, I saw some college girls coming out of a room. They were laughing and I thought about how simple life was back in college. You did not have to worry about anything, unless you wanted to. The biggest things were exams and what to wear to the club. That is a distant memory. Now, it's paying bills or praying I have enough money to pay bills. Gas, food, job and the list can go on and on. They should have had a "life 101"class to prepare us for the real world. Well, I probably would have flunked that course. "Maya, Wait up!" As I turned around, it was Ethan. O my God! I look awful. "Hey Maya," I smiled, but inside, I was wondering if I even brushed my teeth. "You look great! Where are you heading?" he asked. "I'm taking a break from the get-a-long gang and going for a walk," I replied. "May I join you?" he shyly asked, as he drew closer to me. I was like, "Ok." I knew I threw some clothes on to go to breakfast and I was hoping I wasn't funky. As we rode down on the elevator, it was quiet. We smiled, but did not say anything to each other. I wondered what he was thinking. He is fine as can be! Carmel goodness through and through from head to toe sexy mofo! I am horny and hungry at the same time. I did eat a good breakfast, but it went right through me. Damn, Coffee! As the elevator doors opens, we both yelled out at the same time, "So, when you heading out to the football game?" We laughed. I told him, "Probably in a few hours." We don't get there too early, because we are only tailgating. I haven't been to a football game since I was a student at AAU. Ethan looked into my eyes and said, "Maya, I never told you how beautiful you are. I always wanted to go with you, but time was not my friend." I smiled and said "Well, you have a chance if you want it now." His eyes widened as his mouth did. That comment made me realized how single I was and that I wished I would have said it in a sexier way. As we walked, I asked him where John was. He said that he was talking with his fiancé. When I heard that, I knew there was not a chance for Noel to get back with him. "Wow," I said. Ethan turned to me and started talking. Ethan said, "John was crushed by some bitch that avoided him, but Ann was the best thing that happened to him. John did a 180 from the bitch that dumped him." I guess Ethan did not know that Noel was the bitch. I wasn't going to announce it to him, so I just grinned and walked on. "This homecoming is actually his bachelor party. He is getting married next weekend in the Cayman Islands," Ethan announced. I felt so bad for Noel. As we walked, John approached us and said, "Man, I can't wait to marry Ann next weekend. She is so excited!" "Congrats on the wedding," I told him, but in my head, I was thinking about Noel and how she would feel. I hope she can move on, because she doesn't have a choice. "Ethan, I better head back to my room to get ready," I told him. "Ok, Maya. I enjoyed walking with you," he exclaimed. "Take care, John," I called over my shoulder. "You take care too, Maya. See you at the game," he called back. As I walked back to my room, I thought about all the mess that happened in a

24 hour time span. However, things should be getting better, I hope. Walking into the hotel, I saw my ex.

He was talking with someone and was trying to head my way, but I ran into the elevator. I had nothing to say and I wanted to keep it that way. As I get to my floor, the doors open. It's Donald. "Hey Maya, you look kind of tired," he said. "Hey Donald, looking like a jackass," I whispered under my breath. "Maya, sticks and stones like the old saying states," he smirked. I wanted to tell him that if I had a stick or a stone, I would throw it at him. However, I did not have time to entertain donkeys right now. I smiled at him and walked back to my room. As I walked into the room, Noel was sitting on my bed. She looked happy and confused at the same time. Monica was taking a nap. I wish I could have taken one. "Maya, I'm thinking I am going to tell John how I feel. I am going to get him back." Damn, I thought. I wanted to run up to her and shake the crap out of her. However, the only thing that came out of my mouth was "Oh." "Yes," Noel went on saying, "I am going to approach John tonight after the game and proclaim my love to him." "Do you really think that is a good thing?"

I asked, with a questionable look on my face. "Yes, Maya, I messed up and I'm getting my man back! I ran into John earlier and I told him I had something to tell him and he was cool about meeting me." I didn't want to tell her that her love was getting married in the Cayman Islands next weekend. I just didn't feel it was my place to tell her. I wish that it wasn't going to happen, because I came to homecoming for fun and rest. I'm not resting and my fun is looking bad. "You know what I should do," said Noel, "I should go to his room with a coat on and nothing under it." "NO!!!" I yelled so loud that it woke Monica up. Noel, with a puzzled face ask me, "Why don't you think so?" I looked crazy at her, but I didn't want my friend making an ass out of herself. Plus, Noel is a very emotional woman. "Well," I quickly said, "I think that you and John should be in a public area, maybe the bar downstairs." I was thinking to myself that there needs to be witnesses around them. "You're right," she agreed. It would be too much being nude." "Yes, I think it would be better if everyone was fully clothed," I said. "By the way," I asked, "Where is Kim?" They said, "She's in the room with Larry. He got a room here, but it won't be ready till an hour from now. They may be getting it on, we guess." Well, at least someone is getting it on in the right way. My celibacy doesn't bother me, but I wouldn't mind just being held by a man. The feel and smell of a man would be enough to get me through the next 6 months.

"Larry, I love you so much," whispered Kim. "I love you too, Baby," he smiled. "You know, we were supposed to wait till our wedding night. Remember our engagement promise to wait. I missed you and we can make it up by waiting an hour after midnight and it would balance out." "You're crazy, Larry." "Baby, I am crazy for you!" Both of them started kissing again, till someone started knocking on the door. "Kim, I got to start to get ready for the game," said Noel. "I totally forgot about the time," said Kim. "Well," said Larry, "I should be heading downstairs to see if my room is ready. Maybe, you can stay with me tonight to give Noel the chance to have some privacy tonight." Kim giggled, "You're bad, Baby!" Larry grabbed Kim's arm and pulled her up from the bed. He gently kissed her forehead and hand. He looked into her eyes and said, "I love you Kim." He walked towards the door, winked at Kim, and opened the door. Larry said, "I will see you later, Baby doll." She leaped toward Larry shouting," Love you, Larry!" "Kim," said Noel. "I hope you got some matches or scents, because I don't want to smell your love." "Larry and I did not do anything," grinned Kim. Larry is getting a room for tonight and I was going to stay with him, just in case you meet an old friend." Noel smiled, knowing she would be bringing someone back to share her bed.

Chapter Nine

Game Time

As I was getting ready for the game, thoughts of the past experiences at tailgating crossed my mind. The game, the band, free food and drinks, the list can go on and on. Plus, AAU built a large stadium my senior year, which is nice and also a tailgater's heaven. While in the shower, I knew this was the only place I had privacy. I reminisce about the numerous times of getting ready for the homecoming games. It's funny, because before the stadium at our school was built, we had to ride across town to a small and pitiful high school stadium. Once we got there, we always had to sit on the other side, especially if you came late. "Maya!!!!! Your phone is ringing," someone yelled. Damn, can I just get one minute, I thought to myself. I yelled, "Just let it got to voicemail!" Everyone knows I am out of

83

town and I will worry about business on Monday. This was my down time and I am going to enjoy myself. I wonder what is happening in the other room. "It's Ethan!" screamed Monica. I jumped out of the shower and grabbed the phone. I was surprised that I didn't slip on the wet floor. "Hey Maya. It's Ethan. I just wanted to tell you that I got something special for you." I was dripping wet and still needed to go back into the shower. All I could say is, "Ok." Monica was in the mirror curling her hair saying, "Girl, you are sad. You know you could have called him back." I looked at Monica and flicked some water on her, because she knew she could have let the call go to voicemail. "Kim, do you think I will meet someone tonight?" Noel asked as she looked at herself in the mirror. She wasn't the same girl or size in college. Noel sighed and said, "You know I used to be a size 8, but now I'm none of your business." "Child, don't worry about your size," Kim said, "Men don't truly care about size detail. If your booty bounces with your breast, you are fine." As Kim laughs, Noel started to head into the bathroom, wishing, Man, I hope John will take me back. I want to look good for him. I screwed up big time with him. He loved me

84

so much and would have given me the world. However, my fears

destroyed it all. I envy you, Kim. Kim got a man that worships the ground

she walks on. Noel whispered under her breath, "God, if you can grant me

John back, I will give a little more to the church. I will do one better, I will

start going to church more than just on New Year, Easter and Christmas.

Amen."

Kim was thinking about her man and how it's going to be good tonight.

She thought, I promised myself that I was going to wait till our

honeymoon to have sex. Larry is so good. I know it's just going to get

better with time. I'm far from a virgin, but I told Larry that he would have

to be kind with my stuff. It has to be recycled. I'm concerned for Noel,

Kim thought to herself. She is a very beautiful and smart woman, but she

doubts herself too much. How is God going to bring a man to her? She

scares them away before they get close. I am not saying I am perfect, but I

knew when I gave myself a chance to open my heart. God sent Larry and I

thank him every day for that Man. Larry knows I love him. We are like a

reflection of each other. His beautiful smile, lips and hands and how he holds me......I must be horny. Thank goodness I am about to take a hot shower.

Now, what am I going to wear? I thought to myself. As a woman of style, comfort trumps everything. I'm a T-Shirt queen in my sexy jeans. In the past, I wore some high heel boots, and I was in pain the entire time. It was my dumbass trying to look cute and I never did that again! I learned that if you got the booty, nice size breasts and a small waist, you can look good in anything. Monica loves showing her back out. Kim has her own style. Noel, on the other hand, will have AAU hat, shirt, and whatever else can go on her body. We all know in the group who truly has true school spirit. "Maya, I love the Tee," said Monica. I made sure that the jeans came right to the top of my hips and the tee met perfect on my waist. My mom taught me to show off my shape and not the skin. I learned that when you show or give the man everything, he has no reason to purchase the cow, especially if you are giving him the milk for free. I only give them a squirt, so they have to beg for more. As I finished up, the door opens and Noel and Kim came across, ready to go. We were waiting for Monica, as always. Even in college, we would be ready and waiting for Monica. "I'm almost ready," she said, "just finishing up my makeup." I went to the window of the hotel and saw Ethan and John leaving the parking lot. For some reason, I started to think about the mountain near AAU campus. That place was where the college kids would go to make out and look at the city, while making out. I remembered driving up in Ethan's car and talking about something. I truly don't remember what, but I guess it was good. He looked at me with his brown eyes while Tony Toni Tone was playing on the radio. He reached over and gently touched my face. Then he came closer and... "Maya, I am ready!" Monica screamed. Even in a flashback, I get interrupted. We started walking towards the elevator, when Sandra and James came out. Monica smiled at Sandra and they hugged. I smiled, knowing that things will be ok between them. We all headed towards the door laughing and joking about the fun we will be having soon. As the elevator doors open, my ex was there. "Maya, I want to speak with you," he said. I came out and walked toward him. The girls wanted to tell him off, but I motioned to them to go to the car. I asked him,

"What do you want?" As I looked at him, he started to talk, but it sounded like crap coming out. "You look good, Maya," he said. I said, "Thank you." "Why didn't we work out?" he questioned, as he smirked at me. "Well, since you decided to have a child with another woman other than your wife, I wasn't going to tolerate it. You made your decision of what you wanted and I did, as well." He looked up and said, "That's why I cheated on you." I looked at him and wanted to kick him straight in his balls. However, I learned you can't make a whore a husband. "All I wanted was your love and support, but that was asking for too much," I stated. As I started walking to the door, I turned around and said, "I hope you have a good life." From that, I exited the door smiling, knowing everything was going to get better and I was leaving his dumbass in the past. As I walked to the car, Monica ran up to me and gave me a hug. "Are you ok?" she said. I smiled and said, "I'm fine. The past is in back of me and my future lies ahead. Plus, I have a chance for bigger and better things to come." Monica smiled, knowing I was going to be ok. We all got into the car heading toward AAU. Driving to the campus, it was funny to see this small town has grown into something bigger than it was since leaving college. I enjoyed my college years, the good and bad.

Now, I can understand and appreciate all the things I went through to make me the woman I am today. Noel said, "Maya turn up the radio. Remember that song?" It was Luke, "Doo Doo Brown." The SUV was rocking, due to all of us jumping up and down in the car. I would jam to this song in the club. My butt would be in the air. I was very limber then. As we approached the stadium, I could hear the band's horns fill the air. The beating of the drums brought up memories of getting ready for the game, while the band would march through the campus. The sweet, deep-sounding tubas would grab your attention. Reaching the stadium, we all hear the band call out, "Glad to see you again! I haven't seen you since I don't know when. We are the marching Bulldog band. We are the best band, best band in the land!" You could hear a sweet harmony of the music and people singing the song together, while we walked towards the stadium. Homecoming was never about the football team, but the band and tailgating. Majority of the time, we never really knew what team we were playing. As I got closer, I saw a lot of alumni that I had no idea what their names were. I quickly said to everyone, "Yea, girl or boy" in a minute and didn't feel bad about it. Monica and I were clapping with the band, while Noel was looking around for John, since he was going to be tailgating with his frat brothers. Kim was excited and having a good time, since she was the only one in the group that could get some sweet treats afterwards. "Hey Maya," said some guy, "You are looking great!" "Thank you," I said as I smiled back at him. I had no clue what his name was till Kim whispered "Jack" in my ear. I quickly shouted, "Hey Jack, It's so nice to see you." Jack replied, "Yea, I don't get to make it to homecoming that much, but I do enjoy meeting up with friends and future opportunities." I should have noticed that he was licking his lips at me. Well, I know one thing that I don't like men trying to act like L.L. Cool J. Now, that's a sexy man and his wife is lucky as hell. Well, that's one man I probably will never meet unless in my dreams. As we walked on, I spotted Ethan and John with his frat brothers. I noticed Noel started fixing herself up for John. My stomach started to ache, because of the truth I was carrying. "Hey, Ladies!" shouted one of Ethan's frat brother. "Sexy candies are walking this way! Can I have a taste?" It was Nathan "Nasty what?" Jackson. He was known around campus for something he did at a strip club with a dancer, while his friends were right there. There was a song call "Downtown" that described the situation and that's all I have to say about that. "What up, Maya? You look good!" "Thanks, I try to do the best for myself and my body." "Well, let me do something to your body." Nasty laughed as if he was coughing up something awful. "Hello, John," jumped Noel. John came over to Noel and gave her such a deep hug that I felt it. Noel nervously looked around the tent then said, "I wanted to know if you wanted some company later tonight." John looked at Noel, but he knew where she was going with it. He got quiet for a moment and softly said, "Noel, I want to tell you something, but not here." "Ok, but I really want to tell you something, too," whispered Noel. As they look at each other, John's phone rang and he walked away. Noel turned to me smiling, "Everything's ok! Thumbs up!" I wanted to say, "No sweetie, no thumbs up for this situation." As we walked close to the stadium, I saw an

individual that I didn't care too much about in school. Her name is Lisa
Border. She was popular and she had this really real long hair. But, she
looked like the Joker from the Batman movie. We never got along. She
was one of the girls you knew, because of another girl in the group was
cool with her. I remember when she asked me if she would look good with
short hair, I told her yes. However, if she would have done that, she would
have looked crazy as hell with her big eyes and ears sticking out on her
tiny head. Even, Monica said it was wrong for me to have said that. I
didn't like her, so I really didn't care what I said. Homecoming can bring
the best or worst out in a person. Not only are you facing past people or
situations, you are also mixing it with fun and alcohol. You get a big hot
mess waiting to happen. I saw Monica trying to butter up the vendors to
get some free tees and Shea butter. It wasn't just the tube of Shea butter,
but the block of Shea butter. Kim and Noel were walking a little slower
and seemed to be chatting about something. For myself, I was just
thinking about what the band was going to play at halftime and where
could I get some fried fish or BBQ.

"Kim, I am going to make love to John tonight," said Noel with a devilish smile. "I don't know, Noel," Kim said. "How long has it been since you last saw him?" "Well, it's been about two years," Noel said as she looked down on the ground. "Noel, you don't know what could have happened in those two years," frowned Kim. "I know, but I feel the connection we once had," said Noel. "Sweetie, that could be just gas," Kim laughed. Noel stated, "No, it's not, Kim!" "Noel, did you said that John wanted to tell you something too?" asked Kim. Noel eyes started to get wider as she realized what Kim just said. "Oh my Gosh, Kim, he wants me back!" shouted Noel. Kim looked at Noel, but in a way a mother would look at a child when they had too much to eat. "I don't know, Noel," said Kim. "Maybe you need to first see what it is all about. It could be nothing or something, but you got to see first. Promise me that whatever it may be that you will be ok." Kim grasped onto Noel's hand.

I noticed Ethan walking over to me. "Maya, would you walk with me to my truck." I agreed and we started to walk toward the field. Ethan and I talked about some things and laugh too. As we reach the truck, he asked if we could talk for a minute. I was so happy to kind of get away from the crowd to talk to him. He put down the back of the truck, so we could sit down for a moment. "Maya, I wanted to do this for a long time." He slowly raised his hand to my face and gently rubbed my cheek. He kissed me with all the passion a man can place in a simple kiss. All I could say was, "DAMN," in my mind. It's been a long while since I was kissed by a man. Kissed a lot of frogs, but he is higher than them, I hope. I just didn't go around kissing men since my divorce. "Maya, I really want to see if we can make something out of this," said Ethan. Deep down, I wanted to see too, but I try to stay away from Homecoming love. It never lasts and always ends in a bad way. "Maybe, we can take our time and see if something could come of this, but right now, I just want to enjoy you," I told him. We kissed again, and it was nice. "Ethan, you know we need to get back, but we can take our time." We both smiled and just enjoyed this moment in time.

Noel asked Monica, "Have you seen Maya?" "No, but I guess she's with Ethan," said Monica. "Well, I hope to be like that with John tonight,"

94

smiled Noel. "We're going to get it on till the break of dawn!" "It's

Halftime!" Someone shouted and everyone was running towards the

stadium to see both of the bands. It's funny because usually people would

take bathroom breaks or get food during halftime. No Sir, at a Black

college or university, Halftime is Showtime. Everyone will get back to

eating and drinking after the band is back in the stands. Man, AAU came

out of the stands with the drums pounding in the air. Your heart would

follow the beat of the drum. The dancers were not like they use to be when

I was in school. Back in the day, they would be thick, but now they are

thinner than usual. I wanted to be a dancer, but the tryouts were during

summer break. It's not a quick drive from Ohio to Alabama. However,

after hearing about the long practices during the hottest and coldest

months, I was ok not being a dancer. Each section started to walk into

different directions on the field. They would stretch and start to march

high. After the football team started to head off the field, the band would

start to get into place for the halftime show. The drum majors would do

this little dance, run into the middle of the field, and the other four would follow him. He would jump into the air and lands into a split while the others would take note and do the same. It was awesome! The band would shout the school's letters, and then the drums would begin to beat hard, as they marched onto the field. All you can say is awesome!

As, I started walking back with Ethan, I asked him about John and his wedding. "Yea, he is so excited and happy," said Ethan. "I am supposed to be his best man. That is why I brought him here. I wanted to do something different than Vegas or naked ladies. So, I figured out that homecoming had parties and half-naked ladies." As he laughed, I shouted out, "Noel is the bitch." He turned around and looked at me. Ethan looked at me puzzled and said, "What are you talking about?" "Noel is the woman that hurt John. She is the one that didn't return his calls and she is about to confess her love to him," I told him. "Wow!" said Ethan. "I can't let Noel know I told you, but you need to talk with John, because I don't want to spend the rest of this weekend having to deal with drama. "Homecoming is the only time I can have fun. The last thing I need right now are issues," I begged. "Well, Maya, what can I do?" Ethan was puzzled. "You need to leave or something. Get him out of here ASAP," I replied. "Maya, it's not that easy. We are hosting the tailgate party," he said. "Tell everyone you ran out of liqueur and food," I said. "Maya, you know that's impossible," he laughed. "Well," I exclaimed. "I don't know what to do!" "Maya, just let it happen," he said softly, as he reached for my face. "Baby, some things in life, we can't control. John and Noel need to work it out. All you can do is just be there for her." "Yea," I said. "Easy for you to say, you don't know the history of Noel's breakdowns. Noel is my girl and all, but emotionally, she is not balanced. Maybe that is why she has not experienced a healthy relationship. You got to be willing to work for anything in life, including relationships." "Maya, just wait and see what happens," he said, as he gave me a soft kiss on my cheek. For once, I felt hopeful.

Chapter Ten

ALL HELL BREAKS LOOSE

As we walked back to the tent, we noticed that everyone was watching the band, except John. John stayed back, because he didn't go to our school, plus he was watching the drinks and food to make sure no one would grab and dash. "Man, I didn't know when you guys were heading back," said John. "Noel wanted me to go to the stadium to watch the band, but I promised I would stay back to watch the tent." Thank God for perfect timing. I asked, "Hey John, are you happy about your wedding?" John looked at me and said "I know that you are worried about Noel, but that was the past." "She has probably moved on and has a new love in her life." I thought to myself, "Lord please let Noel have a new love somewhere that I don't know about." I saw in the distance, Noel walking fast back to the tent. I was thinking of so many things to say to her so she

98

could avoid talking to John. The sad thing was I was thinking about Ethan kissing me at the truck. Damn, nothing was coming out of my mouth to stop Noel! "John, I really would like to take a walk with you," grinned Noel. John said, "Sure, let me tell Ethan. Hey man, I am heading out for a minute. Can I see the keys to your truck?" Ethan threw him the keys. I wanted to jump in front of them like a volleyball player, but it was too late. Noel smiled at me and I held both of my thumbs up in the air near my face. I was thinking, please don't say anything, Noel, but I just smiled. As they walked away, I just was preparing myself for the downfall of Noel's breakdown.

"John, it's been so long since I last talked with you," grinned Noel. "Yes, it has been a long time," said John. "You look very good and happy," flirted Noel. "Well, God has been good to me over the years. He has blessed me with a lot of happiness and sadness, but I am blessed." Noel was thinking in her mind what she was going to tell him. Noel thought to herself, should I just shout out to him how I feel or not tell him at all? Maybe he moved on? What am I doing? "Is everything alright,"

John asked. "Yes, everything is fine," Noel answered. "Noel, I want you to know that you leaving me hurt me a lot. I didn't know what I did wrong or if it was even me. Over time, I realized that I am happy it happened because........." Noel blurted out, "I WANT YOU BACK, John!" John just stood there. Noel just looked at him puzzled, but he did not say a word. "I know I am stupid for not calling you back or trying not to get in touch with you over the years." "Noel, I don't know what to say," John exclaimed, "but I got to go." He started to walk back to the tent. Noel started to look at the ground so the crowd wouldn't see her tears fall from her eyes. "Ethan, I'm going to head back to the hotel," said John. Ethan asked, "Man, are you ok?" "NO, I just need some time alone." I asked John, "Where is Noel?" He seemed like he was out of it, but he said, "She is walking back, but I got to go now." I knew that all hell was going to break loose. I started out searching for Noel. I knew she would be upset with the news she just heard. As I walked through the crowd, I bumped into Donald. "Oh Maya, in all the places," he grinned. "What, Donald," I looked at him crazy. "I don't have time for you right now, ok." As I

100

picked up the pace to find Noel, I got a text on the phone. "Please come to the car, Noel." I remember how it feels to tell someone you love them and they don't want you. It's painful, but I learned that you can't make anyone love you. It's a process. People over think what love is sometimes. Love is an action. You can say it, but if you don't follow through, it doesn't mean shit. I saw Noel crying near the car. I didn't want to tell her the truth, because it's not my place. Noel was trying to talk, but it's hard to understand someone when they're crying. She said, "Maya, I don't know what happened. John just looked at me as if I was a ghost. I probably knew it was too late, but I wanted to see if I had a chance. I loved him so much, but my fear messed up everything." "Noel, you are a smart woman," I said. "At least he knows now. Sometimes, you got to take a chance at love. I pray to God that I get a chance at love. You know that I never experienced love. Not "I love you," but the love that enters into your soul." Noel was astonished and said, "You mean that your ex didn't love you?" "Hell no, but that's not the point," I looked at her. "Love is not supposed to hurt. You will love again, Noel. The more you learn to love

yourself; God will send you the man that will be attracted to you for you."
She replied, "Maya, I am surprise you don't have anyone else." "Well, I'm
trying to open myself up for love, but I am taking my time," I told her.
"Don't think it doesn't get hard and lonely, but I'd rather be alone than be
with a fool for company." Noel laughed and wiped away the tears. "Well,"
she said, "We still got tonight. Maybe you might meet someone and bring
the joy back." "Where have you two been?" shouted Monica. "We left
something in the car, and I had to get it," said Noel. Monica told us, "I
have been walking around the stadium seeing how people are shocked
about the Sean, aka Sandra transformation. "You know you are wrong,
Monica," I said. "Look Maya, I may be wrong, but I'm keeping it real,"
she replied. I am trying to realize why I came to homecoming, but I know
this will be my last time coming to homecoming. I need a break after all
this shit. With everything going on, I see that Noel is still sad and drinking
a lot. "Hey, take it easy on the quick lick," I said. "Maya," she wailed. "I
put myself out there and he said nothing. What did I do wrong?" I wanted
to tell her so badly that John is getting married next week, but it's not my

place. Someone shouted, "Hey, where is John! You know we are here to celebrate our Frat brother getting married next weekend!" When that guy shouted out that information, I slowly turned around to look at Noel's expression. Her mouth was wide open. I said confused, "Wow, I didn't know that!" I had to play that shit off. "O My God, Maya!" Noel cried. "I feel like a fool. I got to get out of here." "Do you want me to take you back to the hotel," I asked. "No, I will find a way there," she said. After that, she ran out into the crowd. I tried to catch up, but trying to run after a person is different in your 30's. Plus, I didn't want to leave Monica and Kim here without a ride, but I knew that Noel needed a friend right now. So, I asked Ethan if he could borrow one of his frat brother's car to take me to the hotel. He agreed. Once I found Monica and Noel an hour later, I gave them the keys to the car. Ethan and I were walking to the car, knowing I did not want to leave the game. I knew it was getting late and soon everyone would be leaving to get ready for tonight. "Maya, it seems that your day was crazy," replied Ethan. I looked at him and said, "I know." It seems like I have one surprise after another. I was heading back

to find Noel to make sure that she was ok. Then, I am going to take a nap."
"Maya, do you think maybe later we could continue that experience,"
smiled Ethan. Shoot, I wanted to continue it right now, but I needed to be
a good friend right now. We laughed as we drove back to the hotel. I truly
enjoyed Ethan's company. It's been a long time and I am trying to get
back out here dating and it scares the hell out of me. However, love is a
chance that I am willing to take. As we park the car, he turned to me and
gave me the sweetest kiss. "I hope to see you later tonight," he grinned.
"Honey, I will make the time for you," I giggled back. I got out the car
and almost tripped getting out. I looked back and laughed and felt like I
was floating on a cloud. I skipped into the hotel, smiling like I never had
before. I got into the elevator all the while, humming and happy. Walking
to the room, I was skipping like a little girl. As I opened the door, I saw
the most horrible thing! Donald and Noel were in the bed together.
"Maya!" Noel shouted. I was speechless and sick at the same time. I
yelled, "What the hell are you doing!" Donald jumped out of the bed
quickly, trying to put his pants back on. "Maya, you won't tell Kim?"

asked Donald. I looked at him like I was about to kick his ass. I shouted,

"You are crazy! Get out, Donald!" He ran out of the room. I turned back

to Noel and yelled, "What the hell is wrong with you, Noel?" "I was in

pain, and I needed comfort," she cried. I said, "Damn, so you screwed

Donald to ease the pain! I was trying to come back and see about you.

Why didn't you just get drunk! Please tell me you were drunk and that's

why you had sex with Donald? Please say you were drunk!" "No, I was

hurt," Noel said. I could not believe this. I am standing in the hotel room

that smells like the sex of my best friend and my best friend's ex-lover. I

have had more drama in these two days, than in my entire marriage. Noel

asked, "Maya are you going to tell Kim?" I rolled my eyes and said, "Hell

no, that's going to be your job." "Kim must never know! It could destroy

our friendship," cried Noel. "No shit, you just figured that out," I snapped.

Noel continued to cry and said, "Maya, why are you so mean to me?" I

looked at her and thought to myself, is she for real? I had to leave the

room after that comment. I could not put up with Noel crying and the

smell of sex in the room. I closed the door. As I lay on the bed, someone was knocking on my door. It was John. John asked through the door, "Maya, may I come in to talk with you about Noel?" I was wondering was there something on my forehead that said I want to be involved. I got up off the bed and opened the door. "Ethan told me that Noel was upset about my wedding announcement. I will always love Noel," said John, walking toward me. He sat in the chair, looking at the floor. "I needed time to think, since Noel told me that she wanted to be with me." I wondered when Noel saw John. Because of the shock, I forgot that they talked prior to leaving for the game. John got up and walked over to me. "Maya, can you tell Noel to meet me tonight at the bar? I would like to talk with her," he said. "I will tell her, John," as I smiled at him. I got up and walked over to the door to let him out. He turned around and smiled, as he walked away. I walked over to the door in my room and knocked on it. "Come in," Noel yelled. "Hey, John wants you to meet him at the bar tonight," I said. Noel started to cry uncontrollably. "I messed up everything," she murmured. I wanted to agree with her, so I just remained quiet. "Maya, I cannot face John now," she said as she was crying frantically. I was so pissed at Noel, but what could I do? I know that I will not interfere with this situation. What sucks about this situation the most is that I know. I lay on the bed and thought about what went on in the past 24 hours. It's funny because I was laughing even though I shouldn't have. I wanted things to be different, but how was that going to happen? Monica was going to have an affair, but Sean, aka Sandra changed that. Kim is conflicted, even though Larry is here and Noel screwed Donald. This was the worst homecoming I had ever seen, but this situation would be made for television. Maybe once I open my eyes, this could just be an awful dream. For a moment, I went to sleep and dreamed about how simple things were in college. Also, I wondered what would have happened if I never met my ex and would have stayed with Ted. Ted was my friend, but I lost contact with him. He never went to my college, but we met through a mutual friend. He was so cute and he made me laugh. I thought I had met my soul mate, but I guess it was not meant to be.

"Maya, Maya, wake up," said Monica shaking me. "What time is it?" I asked. Monica continued, "Its 6:30. I was checking to see if you wanted to go get some dinner?" I knew I had to get out of here for a moment.

Monica asked me, "Where is Noel?" Kim said, "She is not in her room."

"Well, I don't know, since I fell asleep after checking in on her," I said.

"What is wrong, Maya? I know something is not right because you are

rolling your eyes," Monica said. I hate that Monica could read me. She

could look at my facial expressions and know something was wrong.

"Monica, I've got to tell you something, but you cannot say anything." I

grabbed Monica and sat her on the bed. "Noel screwed Donald," I said.

Monica's face looked as if she ate something that didn't agree with her.

Her eyes got big, but nothing was coming out of her mouth. "Was she

drunk? Please, say she was drunk," Monica stuttered. "She said she was

hurt," I said. Monica looked at me, but nothing came out. "Wow," Monica

grasped. Kim walked into the room. "Man, my room stinks," Kim

laughed. Monica and I just stared at her. "Maya, do you have any

matches?" "Yes," I said. I reached for my purse to give them to her. "I

guess Noel got some relief," giggled Kim. Monica and I both laughed about the situation, but we did not feel that way at all. All I could do was look at Monica and hope Noel was not doing Donald again.

Noel came into the room. She looked down at the floor not to show her eyes. "I don't feel good, and I am going to stay behind," she murmured. Kim gave her a hug and asked, "Do you want us to bring you something?" Noel murmured, "No, I am fine." Kim hugged Noel again and I saw the tears running down her face. I looked at them and Monica just shook her head. "Well, we better be going," I quickly blurted out. "If you need anything, Noel, we are here for you," said Kim. "That's what friends are for," sung Monica under her breath. I gave Monica a look to stop singing. I knew Monica was being a smart-ass. However, I giggled under my breath, as well. As we walked out of the hotel, I was wondering if Noel would ever tell Kim about what she did. I know Kim and Donald have been separated for years, but still it's the principal of the matter. "I hope Noel feels happiness soon," said Kim. "I know she already has," giggled Monica. I bumped Monica's arm to shut her up. Kim turned to me and asked, "Maya, you think Ethan will ask you to have sex?" I thought to myself, "How the hell I would know?" However, I did wonder myself, but I knew as much as I wanted to, I wanted to wait. I'm not a saint, but I'm not a whore either. "Well, I know sex would be bad the first time, so I'd rather wait," I explained. Kim asks, "What do you mean?" "Sex is like learning how to ride a bike. In the beginning, you are falling off, crashing, or looking crazy. After a while, it's smooth and you get to the point of riding fast or slow." All of us laughed because we know it's the truth. Kim asked both of us, "Did you see how Donald was acting at the game?" Monica and I just looked at each other. I was praying that Kim would let it go. She has this fabulous man she is about to marry next summer and she is worried about Donald. "Well, he is an ass!" I exploded. Kim looked concerned and said "Maya, what is wrong? You seem to be acting strangely!" I was thinking to myself how could I tell my best friend that I just saw her ex and Noel humping like rabbits. Just the vision again made me want to vomit. "I'm cool, just starving," I said, with an awful grin. The ride to the restaurant was very long and quiet. I had nothing to say. I was very surprise that Monica wasn't running off at the mouth. Probably, the news I told her kept her silent as well. As we got to the restaurant, Kim's phone rang, "Hey Baby, its Larry." Kim was smiling from ear to ear. "Ok, we are at Mary's. Love you!" said Kim. "Larry is coming to eat with us and he's bringing his cousin," she added. I was so relieved, because this would get Donald off of her mind. The waiter came up and asked, "How many ladies will be in your party?" "There will be five in our party," said Kim. The waiter led us to the table. Kim was talking about the wedding, as I saw Larry come in. Behind him was this beautiful looking man. His skin was golden and his head was bald, but it was shining like the sun. As he was walking to our table, I already figured out our children, where we were living and who would be on top. "Hey ladies, this is my cousin Vincent," Larry said. "Good evening, ladies," Vincent grinned. I was grinning so hard that my face started to hurt. I was so happy that Monica was married. I looked at her like, Ha ha, you can't touch this! She gave me a look like, DAMN, but I'm married. To be honest, I think I heard music in the background, but I realized it was the music in the restaurant. "So, what are you ladies getting into tonight?" asked Vincent. "Well, we are supposed to go out, but I know, I will be turning in early," giggled Kim to

Larry. I wasn't even paying attention to Kim. I was still smiling from

when Vincent walked over from the door. I looked on his hand for rings or

marks on his finger. Thankfully, none were there. "Thank God!" I shouted

out. Everyone looked at me and Vincent smiled. "Just thankful for friends

old and new," I quickly said. "I'm trying to help my cousin find a good

woman to settle down with," said Larry. BINGO! I thought, almost

shouting it out aloud. Vincent smiled at me and I returned the favor. "I am

excited about the wedding next summer," said Larry. "Me too," said Kim.

Larry grabbed Kim's hand and kissed it. I was so happy for Kim. Lord

knows it's hard to find a good person, but once you do hold on and see

what can happen. "So Vincent, Maya is single, maybe you can get to know

one another," said Monica. "Maya is one of the bride maids in the

wedding." I wanted to hug Monica for giving a shout out for me. "Wow,

I'm one of the groomsman in the wedding," said Vincent. I was thanking

God and saying "Wow" at the same time. "Where is Noel?" asked Larry.

"She wasn't feeling well, but we will get her something to go," I told him.

"Well, I hope she gets better," said Larry. Monica and I agreed, but know

the only sickness she is facing is telling Kim the truth. As our food was

coming, Ethan and John came into the restaurant. I was thinking, damn, in

the back of my head. I know a kiss is a kiss, but its homecoming and I

don't know if Ethan was real or not. He did ask for my phone number.

Shoot, Vincent could be in the running for something hopeful in my life. I

don't like to compare guys from my past. I had a guy from my last

relationship that was just talk and no action. Then, he cuts off all forms of

communication with me and disappears from sight. After two years, he

came back into my life like nothing happened. I told him that he was

stupid as hell and I don't go backwards. The ultimate feeling I want is

Love. I have never been in love with a man. I have loved a friend or loved

a guy, but never said, "I'm in love with you." Hell, I did not ever love my

ex-husband! Don't get me wrong, I loved him, but I could hate him in the

same sentence if he pissed me off. I realized that you can love someone

and hate him at the same time. I truly want to know what it feels like to

have someone want and desire me. Vincent gave me a smile and asked,

"Maya, may I ask where you are from?" "I'm from up North, but I currently live down South. I never went back home after college," I told him. He smiled back at me and I was looking at his white teeth that were all there. Plus, he was looking directly at me. I saw John wave at me. I waved back like if I was just throwing my arm up for the waiter. The waiter walked over and asked, "Are you all ready to order?" Since Kim was on her diet, she just ordered a salad and a grilled piece of chicken. Everyone else ordered the food they wanted. "So Maya, you are not going to eat light?" she asked. I don't feel guilty, because I eat healthy all the time. Homecoming is my rest and relaxation so if I want a cheese burger and cheesecake, brings it on! I told the waiter, "I will take a salad too." I knew I would be getting a cheese coney later tonight. "I will bring the bread to the table as soon as possible," said the waiter. I smiled at the waiter, because I had to get additional food from somewhere. "Maya, come with me to the restroom," asked Monica. We both excused ourselves from the table and Vincent actually got up. My eyes were smiling, but all I could say is "Thank you." We walked to the restroom and Ethan waved me over. I walked over and he put a note in my hand. As I opened the note, it said, "Meet me at the bar in the Hotel around Midnight." I smiled and he gave me a wink. As we entered the restroom, Monica turned to me and shouted, "DAMN! Vincent is FINE!" I could not say anything. All I could do is smile. Monica looked down at the paper in my hand. "Girl, what is that?" she asked. I told her that it's from Ethan and that he wanted to meet me at the bar at midnight. Monica started dancing and started singing, "There is nothing wrong with a little bump and grind." I push Monica a little. I knew I wanted it so bad, but I have already been down that road and I wanted a real relationship. No game or sex, but two people that truly love each other. Just getting back in the dating game was hard enough. I was starting to feel like there was no one for me. I remembered before I left my ex, he told me that I would never have someone that would love me like he did. I told him, "Thank God!" "Maya, you deserve to be happy and God will bring the right man to you," smiled Monica. It's great to hear encouraging words, but I still will be going home alone. As we left the restroom, I saw Donald enter the restaurant. I gave him a nasty look, but he just looked at me and put his hand down. I couldn't believe it.

Donald had a conscience. As I walked up to the table, Vincent stood back

up. I just smiled and giggled. "We should bring something back for Noel,

since she is not feeling well," said Kim. I wanted so badly to tell Kim that

the only sickness she has is a heavy guilt on her shoulders. Larry reached

for Kim's hand and whispered something into her ear that made her

giggle. I wished someone would whisper or even yell at me. I envied

Monica and Kim, because it's not easy to be out here single. There are

some crazy-ass men out here. Also, the good men get messed up by crazy-

ass women. The tide can go both ways. There may be some good men, but

I haven't seen or met them yet. Everyone tells me that it's better to be

alone, but it's usually the ones who already have someone to go home to.

All I have at my house is a beta fish and a futon. What makes it worse is

that I have been going through a lot of beta fish. They keep dying on me.

I'm on my third one now. "Maya, what are you doing tonight," asked

Vincent. I quickly snapped back to reality. "Oh, just going with the flow,"

I said. "Vincent and I are going wherever you go tonight, Kim," said

Larry. Kim eyes lighted up because this is more time with her man. Shoot, I don't blame her one bit. If I had a man, I would spend as much time as I could. The waiter came back to the table to see if we were ready for our checks. "Could you please bring a menu? I need to order a plate to go," asked Kim. I looked at Monica and I saw her eyes roll deep in the back of her head. As I looked up, I saw Donald approach the table. I could not believe how bold he was. Larry never met Donald. He just knew him by the stories from Kim. "Hey Kim, Monica and Maya," said Donald. "I'm Donald," as he introduced himself to Larry. Larry got up. I thought to myself, he was either going to be a gentleman or kick his ass. Larry reached out his hand towards Donald. "I'm glad to meet you, Donald," said Larry. All of us at the table could not believe it. Larry said, "I want to thank you for messing up, because it allowed me to show Kim how a true man should treat a woman." He sat back down and Donald could not say anything. Kim grinned her ass off. The waiter came with the checks, but Larry took them all and said, "Dinner is all on me." I started grinning as well. "Maya, can I speak to you?" I excused myself from the table and told them I would meet them outside. I looked at Donald with a glance of not

being happy with him. The walk outside to speak to him was as cold as the

weather outside of the restaurant. "Maya, please tell Noel I want to talk

with her," asked Donald. I couldn't believe my ears. First, he acted like an

ass to me, treated Kim like crap, screwed Noel and then grew a heart!

"Maya, I know that I am not the best person, but when Noel came to me, I

had to comfort her," he said solemnly. I looked at him and realized that

this could not just be the first time. I slowly said to him, "Donald, how

long have you and Noel been seeing each other?" He quickly stated, "Noel

and I've been seeing each for over six months now." I was shocked as

hell! He was acting just to keep up appearances. "Maya, I love Noel, but it

hurt me that she had feelings for John. I wanted to show her how much I

loved her and have always loved her," Donald said. I could not believe my

ears. I'm thinking to myself that Donald may have cared about Noel since

college. I asked, "Donald did you mess with Noel in college?" "No. I was

with Kim because I thought Noel would never talk to me. I admired her

drive and passion. She would never want to be with me, especially dating her friend," admitted Donald. I felt sick to my stomach hearing all this news. What made matters worse was that he's honest about his feelings toward Noel. Donald's eyes were watering and he asked again, "Maya, please tell Noel to call me." I looked up at him and rolled my eyes. However, I am a sucker for love. I truly didn't want to get involved with this so called love triangle, but it had to be done. I said, "Yes, I will tell her." Donald smiled. Everyone came out of the restaurant, and he walked away. Vincent came up to me, and asked, "Are you ok, Maya?" I became deaf to him, because all I could think about was that Donald loved Noel. "Maya, are you ok?" I looked up at him and smiled. "Yes."

Chapter Eleven

Tonight is the Night

Kim decided to ride back to the hotel with Larry and Vincent. I was confused about everything that was going on. The ride back was quiet, and I wanted so badly to tell Monica what I knew. I don't want to be the only one who knew it all. I told Monica, "I loved how smoothly Larry told Donald off." "Yea, girl, he gave it to him," laughed Monica. Kim is so sweet, but I know she has a side that will kick your ass if you piss her off. Well, at least Larry showed her how much he loves and respects her. Monica asked, "Maya is everything ok?" I was still debating on telling her about the Donald and Noel love triangle. I came to the conclusion that I did not want to be alone in this mess. I looked at Monica and before I let it out, my phone rang. "Hello," I said. "Don't forget about our midnight meeting, Maya," said Ethan. I totally forgot, but all I could say was "Ok."

After that, I decided to tell her later. We finally got back to the hotel. As I sat in the car, I realized I knew all of Noel's mess. If Kim finds out about Noel and Donald, I don't know how she will feel about both of them. Monica stared at me and asked, "Maya, what's wrong?" I turned to Monica, but nothing came out. Monica said, "Girl, just say it!" "Noel and Donald have been going together for six months now," I blurted out. Monica looked at me with her mouth wide open. She shouted, "What the hell? What the hell? What the hell?" She kept saying it. I just rolled my eyes, because I now regret telling her. "I cannot believe that Noel could go with Donald, knowing everything that he did to Kim," said Monica. Monica turned to me and said, "So how do you feel?" I just shook my head. I opened the car door and quickly jumped out. I did not want to talk about Monica, Kim or Noel's problems. This was homecoming. I came to have fun and relax this weekend, but No! I am getting tired of this crap. I have enough mess in my life. Shit, all of them have drama and a man. I have peace and I'm alone. After thinking about that comment, I thank God that I have a peaceful life. However, I do want to be in a healthy and loving relationship one day. Today would be great, but it will happen when it happens. Instead of me going to the room, I went straight to the bar. I'm not a drinker, but I need one so bad. The bartender came up to me and asked, "What drink would you like, Madam?" "Make it a Cosmo," I said. "Can I join you?" I turned around and it was Sandra. "It looks like there is a lot on your mind, caramel child," said Sandra. I wanted to tell Sandra all that was on my mind, but I felt that this was not the time or place. "Sandra, I wanted a drama-free weekend," I said, while sipping on my drink. Sandra dramatically expressed, "Well, I learned in life that you got to take a breath and blow it out like crazy." "Honey, these battles are not yours! Whatever you are going through, you got to say, "Hell to the no and let it Go!" Sandra got up from the bar stool, and turned to me. She positioned herself like she was going into battle. "Maya, you put out your hand and snap your neck," she said. As I watched her, I felt empowered. However, I knew that I had so much crap on my mind and I had to dump it. I said, "Sandra, I truly appreciate your "Go Girl" thing, but I do have a lot on my mind and I need a drink." "Well, since I am here, I will be happy to join you. Honey, I need a break anyway," giggled Sandra sipping

on some beer. "James is wearing me out!" Sandra said, "I developed new

muscles all over my body!" I looked at her like I was happy and pissed at

her at the same time. "Oh sweetie, I am sorry! How long has it been?"

asked Sandra. "Almost two years," I said. "Damn, Oh, what I meant was

that's good, sweetie. You will be blessed," Sandra said. I told her I wasn't

practicing celibacy. I kind of fell into it. "Maya, you are a beautiful and

intelligent woman," she said. I knew this, but I wanted someone else to

know this too. "Sandra, I want a relationship," I said. "I have tried online

dating, speed dating, match up, casual run-ins, church, etc.... and I seem

to meet the craziest men through all those channels." "Maya, since I was a

man, I will say that you have not met your reflection," she said. I looked at

her in confusion. "Your reflection will be everything you are, but it will be

in that man. One thing I know is when you meet him, you will know. It's

hard to describe, but he will know as well. Your ex-husband did not know

how to love himself and that is why he did not know how to love you.

Even if he is with that other woman, he will never truly love her because true love holds no lies." Sandra quickly swallowed her beer and gave me a

hug. "Maya, one day you will be so happy. Believe and keep moving

forward toward it." As she walked away, I thought about everything she

said. I cannot worry about the past or the future. My main focus was now

and what I was going to do about it. I got up from the bar and said

"Charge it to Room 215." Shoot, if I had to hold Noel's situation, she

could at least pay for my drink. As I walked to the elevator, I was in deep

thought. Ethan surprised me by quickly popping up behind me and placing

his arms around my waist. I wanted to just fall into his arms, but I had to

play it off. I gently pushed him away, but he grinned at me. As the

elevator opened, a couple walked out and we walked in. I turned around as

the doors closed and he grabbed me. He looked into my eyes and kissed

me so softly that I felt my stomach jump. He looked at me and said, "I

think you need some stress relief." I could not say anything, but shake my

head. He pushed the floor button and took my hand. Ethan kissed my hand

and gave me a look that made me wet. I was happy, because the drought

may be over. However, I was thinking that I did not have condoms, because I wasn't planning on have sex. Honestly, I didn't want to have sex because I like him, but not "like him, like him." Shit, I want it, but I'm tired of easy come, easy go relationships. I want a husband. I want to be recycled! By the time, I finished talking to myself in my head; we were already in his room. He laid me on the bed after he removed the top blanket, because we have all seen the news specials with the blue light. He kissed me so deeply and passionately. Man, I needed this stress relief. As he tried to take off my pants, I asked him if he had a condom. He stopped and pulled it out of his coat pocket. "Maya, I want you so bad," he moaned. Deep down, I wanted this man to jump my bones, but I wanted more than just sex. "Ethan, I think we should wait," I hesitated in saying this. He kissed my neck, and looked into my eyes. He said, "I waited this long, but I am willing to wait a little bit longer for you." We both grinned and kissed each other. He got up and reached down to help me up. He hugged me so tight that I felt my breath leave my body. "When that time comes, I want to do more than have sex, I want to make love to you," he explained. I wanted so badly to tell him that I probably will not make love with him because I don't love him. I like him. Maybe we can make like together. Ethan grabbed my hand and asked, "What is on your mind?" I looked down, because I know I wear my emotions on my face. I could not play if off, even if I could. "Maya, I know something is wrong," he said. I just don't feel that Ethan needs to get into the mess I am in. I just decided to kiss him, so I could stop him from asking me anymore questions.

"Noel, I got you some food," said Kim. "Thanks Kim," moaned Noel. She looks at the food, but with the guilt in her mind, the food did not look tasty. "Noel, I am sorry about John, God will bring you someone good," she smiled. Noel knew she was wrong, but how could she clear her conscience and maintain her friendship with Kim. Kim has always been there for Noel. If I needed something, Kim would have it. I slept with the love and hate of her life. Maybe I should tell her and she would forgive me. Or, maybe she could kick my ass. I don't know with Kim. I've seen her pissed at someone. It's not pretty. "Noel, are you ok? It seems like you are in deep thought," asked Kim. "No, just thinking about something important," she replied.

126

"Hey Ladies, we need to start getting ready for the party tonight," said Monica. Kim looked around and asked, "Where is Maya?" "She decided to get a drink at the bar," said Monica. Monica looked at Noel with a funny glance. Noel realized that Monica knew about the situation. "Kim, could you excuse us? I need to speak with Monica," said Noel. Monica and Noel walked into the other room and closed the door. Noel turned around and said, "I don't believe Maya told you!" whispered Noel. "I can't believe you had sex with Donald!" Monica walked closer to Noel. "You know what Donald took Kim through," whispered Monica. "I know I am wrong, but I was hurt and he comforted me," she whined. "So the hell what? You slept with our best friend's man!" Monica was trying so hard to keep her voice down. "Monica, you were going to sleep with Sean," said Noel. Monica rolled her eyes and said, "Well, you know that was not going to happen now! Yes, Noel, I was going to do wrong, but I did not screw one of your past men," yelled Monica. Noel said, "Look, I know I'm wrong and I could mess up my friendship with Kim, but I am going to tell her." Monica turned to go back into the other room. She

127

turned around and said, "If you have a conscience and believe in karma, you better tell her because it may come back." Noel turned to Monica and asked, "Are you going to tell Kim?" "Hell NO! That is not my place," said Monica and walked into the room.

Noel sat on the bed and her heart sank in her chest. A knock came at the door. She didn't want to talk to anyone, but she wondered who it could be. As she approached the door, she looked in the peep hole. It was John. Noel's eyes jumped out of her head! She ran to the mirror to wipe the tears from her eyes and fixed her hair. She shouted, "I'm coming." Noel opened the door and smiled. "Hello," she calmly tried to say. "Hello Noel, you look good," said John. "I wanted to talk with you, if you have the time," he smiled. Noel knew that her mind was not there with everything that had happened earlier, but she wanted to see what he had to say. John walked into the room and sat on the chair near the desk. Noel closed the door and sat on the bed that was kind of far away from him. "Noel, I knew that I loved you. I wanted to marry you, but I guess you did not feel the same," he said. "I am happy now and about to marry a great woman. She kind of reminds me of you." Noel could not get mad with his comment; because she knew she stopped the relationship. "John, I am sorry for ignoring you," said Noel. "It was so wrong of me, but I thought I would have a second chance. I guess I am too late." John came over to the bed next to Noel. He grabbed her hand and kissed it. John said, "You showed me so much about love, Noel. I just wanted you to know that you deserve love and shouldn't let it pass you by," smiled John. Noel said, "I let you get away, because I put my career in front of you and now I am alone." John got up and pulled Noel close to him and said, "Don't say that, you will have love sooner than you think. You have to first love yourself and want someone in your life," he said. He also continued saying, "Don't give up, but don't be the man either." Noel got upset and pushed John away. "I wasn't trying to act like a man," she yelled. John grabbed her hands and looked into her eyes. "What I meant was to allow the man to be the man, because he will give you what you need as his woman." Noel gave John a puzzled look. John explained again, "If you do everything in the relationship, then what would he be good for? Let him do his part and he

129

will give balance to your life. You cannot always do it alone. You deserve a helpmate." Noel remembered what her mother and father told her about having someone help you. She was so scared to allow the man to do anything because of the relationship her parents had. She felt like if she was in control, he would not control her. "Noel, I understand what your father put your mother through," explained John. "Not every man wants to control you. There are some good men out here. You have to be willing to see them with your head and heart, sweetheart." Noel had not heard John call her that name in years. A tear dropped from Noel's eyes. John gently wiped her eyes. Both of them started to glance at each other which turned into a deep stare. Noel started to lean towards John, but he turned his head. "I'm about to get married and I love my future wife," John said. Noel walked to the door. "I think you better go, John," whispered Noel. John got up off the bed and walked toward the door. Before he could get there, Noel jumped into John arms and kissed the heck out of him. John was shocked, but he did not stop her. Once it was over, Noel said, "At least, I got to kiss you goodbye!" John was speechless. Noel opened the door and John walked out and she closed the door.

Noel's back hit the door hard, as she slid down it. She fell to the floor and began to cry. As she got into at deep cry, I opened the door. I did not know she was there, but I knew I knocked the hell out of her. I softly giggled and said, "Oh Noel, are you ok?" "Yes, I am ok," said Noel. As I walked into the room, I saw that Noel was crying again. I didn't want to ask, but Noel started talking to me. "Maya, why is this happening to me?" Noel got off the floor and ran to the bed and fell down on it hard. To be honest, I did not want to say anything. I was tired and I didn't even want to get into anything that just happened. So, I turned my head and rolled my eyes. I said, "Noel, I don't know what to say about today." I really could not comfort her about John getting married or screwing Donald. I walked into the other room where Monica and Kim were sitting. Both of them were laughing over something. "Hey, Maya," said Kim. "I thought you got lost on the way back to the room!" I just nodded my head. "Is Noel ok?" asked Kim. Monica and I looked at each other. "Yea, she is fine," said Monica. I hit Monica, because she rolled her eyes when she walked away. Kim said, "Vincent said that you were cute." I felt like it was a compliment from sixth grade. I was ready to hear if he likes me or "like me, likes me." I smiled but, I did not know what to say. "Maya, I mean that he finds you very attractive," laughed Kim. Monica said, "We need to start to get ready for tonight." "Kim, you start getting ready and we will check on Noel," said Monica smiling. As Monica and I walked into the other room, I closed the door so Kim would not hear us. As we both walked into the room, Noel was still lying on the bed. Monica and I both looked at each other and sat on the bed across from her. Monica couldn't do anything, except roll her eyes. I said, "Noel, you better start getting ready to go out." Noel looked up at us and said, "I can not go!" Monica got up and said, "I love you, but you better get your ass up." Noel just looked up in shock. To be honest, I was shocked myself. "Noel, you screwed Donald and John is getting married, so boohoo!" My eyes just keep getting bigger. "Monica!" said Noel. Monica continued, "Look, you better play it off and fake it till you make it, sweetie. I didn't come all the way to Homecoming to hear drama bullshit. You are not the only woman going through man issues. You will probably be going through this shit until you die." "But, Monica! I don't want to go!" Noel jumped up from the bed and ran to the bathroom. She came back with a pregnancy test in her hand. I was thinking to myself, "Where in the hell did she get a test from?" "I'm pregnant," said Noel. Monica just stood there in shock. Noel ask, "Maya, how do you feel?" I looked at her and then at Monica. I turned around quietly and walked out the door. I keep walking down the hall to the only person I could talk to in college. I knocked on the door and a voice said, "Who is it?" I could not say a word. As the door opened, Sandra looked at me. "What is wrong?" she said. I just looked at her like someone just cut out my tongue. All I could do is the gesture for drinking. She already knew what I meant. Sandra turned her head and said, "James, I'm heading to the bar!" He said, "Ok." As the door closed behind her, I was wondering why all of this was happening now. Don't get me wrong, I love Noel like a sister, but I wanted to kick her ass. She is book smart, but common sense, I realized, was never her strongest point. As we got off the elevator, I saw Donald out of the corner of my eye. I wanted to run over to him and kick him in the balls so hard. However, I realize now why his actions were changing, because Noel probably told him she was pregnant. It's all starting to make sense. The bartender said, "Back so soon ladies? What would you both like to drink?" Sandra said, "It will mostly depend on what will come out of my friend's mouth." Sandra turned to me and asked what happened. I turned to face her and said, "Noel is pregnant." Sandra smiled and said, "This is a celebration! Champagne all around, baby!" boosted Sandra. The bartender nodded his head. "She may be having Donald's baby," I whispered. Sandra quickly shouted to the bartender, "Honey, change that order! Two shots of Jack! What the fu**!" said Sandra. "Maya, please say Donald Trump or Donald Duck, but not Kim's ex-Donald!" Honestly, I didn't know if it was Donald's, but I bet it is. "Two double jacks," said the bartender. I said, "That's ok, I don't drink that." Sandra looked and said, "These are for me." She grabbed both drinks and slammed one down. I just told him to make me a Shirley Temple. There was a silence between both of us. With the second drink,

Sandra just sipped on it. Now, I have to deal with knowing, not only had Noel been having sex with Donald, but now she could be carrying Donald's baby. Sandra just looked at me and said, "You know that Kim is going to kick Noel's ass." Kim is like two people. She is sweet, but if you piss her off, she is mad as hell. Both of us know what Kim is capable of. I never want to get on her bad side. Donald brought it out of her when she was graduating from college and he never showed up. Now, he showed up the night before and got some. Donald made a lot of promises to Kim, but his promises were not worth shit. "Maya, you can't say a word to Kim," explained Sandra. That is Noel's job, I thought to myself. "Well, at least I will be at the wedding, because Kim invited me," said Sandra. I am excited, because now I will have more people to have fun with. I am so ready for Kim's wedding, since it's going to be a destination wedding. I made sure to save my money, because I have been struggling for a while, since my divorce. Sandra gave me a big hug. "Sweetie, God got someone so special for you," she said. I embraced her, because I felt like I was back in college when I would talk with Sean. He, now she, would always be supportive. We both just sat quietly for a moment then Sandra said, "You

got to go back upstairs and get ready to go out." I looked at her and

smiled. I knew she was right. I wanted to go out, because this was the right

thing to do. I don't need to act funny now. So, I got up and left Sandra at

the bar. As I walked towards the elevator, I knew that I had to shake it off

and be there for Kim and all the girls. Regardless of the situation, I have to

be there for Noel as well. As the doors open, I saw Donald standing at

Noel's door. I yelled out, "Donald!" He quickly turned around and saw

me. My eyes popped out of my head and I told him to come here. "What?"

Donald asked. I quickly went up to him and pointed my finger at him.

"Look, you need to talk with Noel at a later time," I said. He looked down

at the ground and was quiet. Donald looked up and said, "I want to do

what is right, Maya. I want to be there for my child and Noel." "Well, I am

happy you want to do that, but why now, with Kim here?" I explained.

"Shoot, in the beginning, you were trying to break up what Kim had, now

you're acting like a gentleman," I giggled. Donald put his hand on his

temple and massages it. Then, he said, "My child deserves a father, I did not have that. Maybe if I saw it in my life, I probably would have been better to Kim. I can't change what I did to her, but I can make it up to Noel." In my mind, I was thinking that he was full of shit. However, I will never question a man who wants to be in his child's life. I looked up at him and said, "Tell me what room you're in and I'll have Noel come see you." Donald smiled and said, "I'm in room 211. Thank you, Maya," said Donald, as he quickly walked back down the hallway. I rolled my eyes and took a deep breath and walked toward the door. As I opened the door, Monica looked at me and quickly came outside. "Is Donald gone?" she asked. I shook my head yes. She said, "Girl, I lied to everyone that no one was knocking at the door." "Shoot, I said you forgot your key," laughed Monica. "Donald wants to see Noel because he wants to be in the baby's life," I told Monica. Monica rolled her eyes and said, "This is going to be a lot of mess when it comes out. I agreed with Monica, but I also know that I will not be the one telling her this. It's not my place. It's Noel's. "Maya, I am not going to say a word, but we both need to talk with Noel tomorrow," explained Monica. I agreed. I knew I better start to get ready for tonight. I never thought that I would get to the point that I did not want

to go out. I felt bad for Kim and Noel. I never thought that I would have to

choose between both of my friends. Noel is wrong for what she did, but I

know she needs us now, more than ever. Monica came in the room with

me and said, "I really don't want to go now, but I paid all this money for

the plane ticket, the room, the fine clothes and gym expense to get my

body right in order to have a good time. At this point in the game, I wasn't

listening to anyone anymore. I was just drowning out sound, because I

couldn't take it anymore! Between Sandra, Monica, Kim and Noel, I

wanted to just pack my bags and leave this whole situation. I knew this

would be the last homecoming I would be coming to for a while, because I

needed a break. I guess God made sure to end this one with a bang. At

least, I forgot all the crap I was going through! I was standing in the

bathroom, looking at myself in the mirror and remembering simpler times

at college. Yes, it was a simpler time than what is going on now. I was still

living on my parents, even though there were two states between us. It's

funny when things happen in your life, because you think it couldn't happen to you, but it can. You can love someone that never, ever loves

you, but they would just settle due to obligation. I don't want obligational

love. I want a man to desire me more than air and water. I know it sound

crazy, but I know you need both and that's what I want to be to him. I

looked down at my phone and a text came over. It's Ethan, and he sent me

a reminder of our meeting at midnight. I smiled, because I am now just

enjoying the moment. Monica walked into the bathroom and leaned her

head on my shoulder and made her sad dog eyes look. She would always

do that in college if she needed me to help her with something. I would tell

her no, but she would say "please" all day until I would just say fine. I

said, "What do you want, Monica?" "I need to borrow some money for

tonight, because I lost my cash at the tailgate, PLEASE." I rolled my eyes

so hard, my head started to hurt. I said, "How did you lose your money

since tailgating is free?" "Pleasssssssssssssssssssssssse," yelled Monica. I

started to drown her out, until my cellphone rang. I smiled and answered

the phone, because I knew she would have to be quiet. "Hello, Maya

speaking," I said. "It's Ethan. Hey baby." I smiled a little, because I thought "baby" was kind of too soon, but after that kiss, it was fine with me. "I wanted to reach out to you to tell you that you were on my mind. I just wanted you to know that," he said. I smiled and Monica just looked at me crazy, because she didn't know who I was talking with. Good! It wasn't any of her business to know it was Ethan. "Well, baby, I will see you at midnight, love." "See you later, E," I said and hung up. Monica grinned at me and asked, "Who was that?" I just smiled and kept on applying my makeup. "Yes, I will give you the money for tonight, but you buy me breakfast in the morning. I saw an ATM machine in the lobby downstairs," I said. Monica agreed and started to put on her makeup, as well. We both were in the bathroom when we heard a knock at the door. We both looked at each other because we did not want to get the door. However, once we heard her loud voice, we knew who it was. "One of you divas needs to come to the door because I got some stuff to say!" I knew it was Sandra, so I walked to the door. Yes, it was Sandra. "Hey, I got some news for you, boo," she said. "Kim asked me to be in the wedding as a bride's maid. Monica stuck her head out the bathroom door and rolled her eyes. I just smiled and said, "Congratulations!" "Honey, I am so excited about being one!" Sandra screamed. "Now, close the door, because I got some shit to tell you," she whispered. I quickly closed the door to the hallway and the door to the other room that Kim and Noel are sharing. "I don't believe in gossip, but I believe in the truth, good or bad," said Sandra. "However, I was in the hallway and Donald was talking with one of his frats and said that he truly loves Noel and wants to be with her. Now, on top of that, Kim still has no idea that Noel was in the bed with Donald, right?" Monica came out of the bathroom with her mouth wide open. "Maya! You were supposed to keep it to yourself. It's not good to lie!" Both Sandra and I looked at her, since we both know she came to have sex with Sean, now Sandra, in the first place. "Honey, tomorrow is Sunday and you can drive by a lake and purify yourself there," laughed Sandra. Monica rolled her eyes and walked back into the bathroom. "Maya, I don't think it is right to keep this from Kim," said Sandra, with a serious look on her face. I walked toward the bed and sat down to get off my feet. I looked up and stated, "It's none of our business." Sandra put her hands on her hip while Monica came out of the bathroom trying to be nosy. I looked down at the floor and was thinking hard about everything, but all I know is that it was between Noel and Kim. I know that everyone comes to me for help and guidance, but sometimes, I just want to be left out of it. Hell, I got my own problems. I'm tired of being the one in the middle to make things better. Shit, we are grown-ass people. I got up off the bed and walked into the bathroom to continue to get ready. Sandra and Monica looked at each other and Sandra said, "Thank God, I'm a woman now, because this would be uncomfortable." Monica agreed.

Noel was sitting at the bar and wondering what she was going to do now. She was sipping on water, since she will not be able to drink for a while. She realized that the case of fine wines she purchase will now be gifts she will be handing out to her friends at Christmas. It was wrong for what she did to Kim. The fact that her friend doesn't know is driving her crazy. She is the maid of honor in Kim's wedding and she betrayed her. She was thinking of so many ways to try to tell Kim, but what could she do? She just sat there in her pain, not knowing if this will end her friendship and sisterhood with Kim. "I don't think you should be drinking in your condition," said a voice. Noel quickly turned around and saw Donald. "It's water," she said quickly. Donald sat down beside her and gave her a look that showed concerned. "Noel, you know that I love you," he said. She looked around and held her finger to his lips. "Baby, I'm just telling you how I feel," Donald whispered, as he touches her hand. Noel knows it was wrong, but she deeply cared for him, as well. They both looked at each other without speaking a word. "Noel, I have been in love with you since college and the only reason you did not want to talk with me was because I talked with Kim first. Noel said, "She is my friend and we all had a code in college that we would not talk with each other's man." Donald looked around and said, "I wanted to be your man, but you did not give me a chance. I have been treating you like a queen, since we have been together and now you are pregnant with my child. I want to be a father to our child and a husband to you." A tear came down from her eye. She finally had someone who loved her, but it was a man that showed disrespect to her friend. Noel looked down at the glass and spoke, "I don't know if I can lose Kim as a friend." Donald got up off the seat and said, "Regardless of how you feel, I love you and I am going to be in my child's life." He walked away, shaking his head and Noel's phone began to ring. "Hello, this is Noel," she said composed. "Hey, it's Maya, where are you?" She was quiet for a moment and told me that she was at the bar. I told her that we will be ready in a minute to go out to the party for the grown and sexy. Noel just said, "Ok."

As I hung up the phone, I heard the door open. It was Kim with a great big smile on her face. She was humming a song and grinning from ear to ear. Monica said, "I know who had sex!" Kim just said, "I didn't have sex, girl. I made love!" Both of them gave a high five. I rolled my eyes, because I have not done anything since my divorce. Then Kim said, "Just playing! Nothing happened." Monica grabbed Kim's hand and told her that she was taking her high five back. I realized that single sex and married sex are two different experiences. Single sex is awful and married sex is great. Since my divorce, I've had sex, but it was not enjoyable. First, the emotions were not there for me. It's funny, because those guys think they're great, but I never go back with them after it happen. (Hint, hint.) Lord, knows I need a tall glass of water, but I seem to get squirt bottles. I actually have been celibate for a while, which is not bad until Ethan kissed me and now, my body has awaken from a coma. Men have it easy. They can think of someone and hand jive a few minutes and they're good. With women, it is first thinking about a guy we like, and then coming up with an idea to put ourselves in a romantic place. However, by the time we do all of that, we have to make sure the bullet has batteries and then you find out that they are dead, so you just wasted 20 minutes of thinking. Yes, I am mad because I finally got a good one, but that's what happens when you try to get yourself off. So, I am just waiting till the right man comes because it's been two years. As Monica and Kim enjoyed talking about sex, I went back into the bathroom to finish getting ready. I heard the door open and it was Noel. Kim ran over to Noel and hugged her and said, "Congratuations, we need to get you a special dress since you will be bigger when my wedding comes around." Noel just smiled, because deep down she wanted to cry. "Yes, I don't know how far I am, but I bet the dress will need to be wider," she stated. As I went over to the other room, I heard Kim singing in the bathroom. As I walked up to the door, Kim just came up to me and said, "Maya, I wanted to do something with Larry so bad, but he sang to me!" I just smiled and said, "Great." I truly was happy and didn't care at the same time. "Noel is pregnant and I am getting married! Great news is coming from everywhere," Kim expressed excitedly. Monica and I just looked at each other, because deep down we are happy for Kim's news, but not so much for Noel's. "I better start getting ready for tonight," I said. Everyone looked at me and Monica said, "Maya, you have already been ready!" I looked in the mirror and she was right. I have been dealing with all of the girls' crap that I didn't pay attention to what I was doing. So, I just walked over to the bed and sat down and waited on the girls to finish.

As we left the room, I saw Sandra and James walking down the hallway. Sandra spoke, saying, "Too fine as wine and too rich for you bitches!" I just smiled and thought that she had a lot of catch phrases. Anyway, I was excited and was thinking about going out, but I saw

Donald coming out of his room. I totally forgot telling Noel about what he said. I did not want to make it obvious, so I put up my middle finger at him and said, "Well, we'll see about that man!"

That was the only thing I could come up with on a quick notice, because I did not want Kim to think I had changed my feelings for him. I winked and turned to Noel and asked her for a personal item. Kim said, "I got a Tampon that you can have." I told her, "No, I like Noel's, because of the flowers and stuff." I grabbed her hand and led her to the other room. I took her into the bathroom and said, "Donald wants you to talk with him in his room." Noel looked down at the ground and was silent. "Look, I'm just the messenger," I whispered. "Maya, I have nothing to say to him." I looked at her crazy. "Honey, you are going to see what this man had to say. You have been seeing him for almost six months and probably carrying his child. You are far from being the helpless soul," I tried to keep at a whisper. "Fine," Noel pouted. Monica yelled out, "Come on, I know it didn't take this long to get a pad!" I opened the door and we both tried to walk out at the same time. I said, "We are ready." I opened up the door to get out of the room, Larry and Vincent was right at the door. "Good evening Ladies," said Larry. Kim was smiling like crazy. "Maya, you look very beautiful," Vincent smoothly expressed. I just smiled, as well. Shoot, I was going to have a good time tonight, because this was the last night. We all walked to the elevator and everyone was looking sharp. If we all had theme music, we would be Outkast's "So fresh, so clean." All of us got into the elevator and made it to the main floor without any issues or situations. I started to get excited and the weather was wonderful that night. Larry and Vincent walked us to our cars and opened the doors like gentlemen. Larry took Kim's hand and kissed it and said, "See you later, mi Corazon." Everyone in the car just went crazy. Monica said, "Your man could say fried okra and it would probably sound sexy as hell." We all laughed because it was true. The ride to the club was fine. I was waiting for all hell to break loose, but it didn't. Even Noel started to talk a little, but there was still an air of mess from earlier. Our college town was small and pitiful when we were here some years ago. It has truly grown in the years since we have left. Even our campus expanded, because I remembered we had a train track in front of our Gym. We were laughing about the panty raids and the time that Monica and Kim were in a water fight and were scared to death about getting attacked again.

They ran to the back of the building in all that high grass. They had to run with their legs high in the air for fear of snakes or other animals that could be in the grass. We finally got to the parking lot and saw the people walking up to this beautiful building. Noel was walking kind of slow. I told Monica and Kim to walk on and we would catch up with them as soon as we can. "Maya, I am scared about having this baby and maybe losing Kim as a sister," Noel sighed. I did not know what to say, because I don't have children and I never slept with any of my friend's men. I turned to her and said, "I got your back with it all. I don't know what Kim is going to say or do, but for now, just enjoy the moment." Noel tried to smile, but she just nodded her head. We stood in line and waited. I was happy, because out of nowhere, people were forming a line behind us. Once we got to the door, this tall, country-looking dude said, "It will be $20 dollars, ladies." Man, Kim was going off, saying it was too much money. Monica said, "You do this every year about the money. You know they are going to get what they can. I'm going in." Kim caved in like always, but she always enjoyed herself. Once in, the place was big and beautiful inside. There were two levels in the building. The sad thing was that all the years going to school here, I've never heard of this place. They had a really big dance floor at the bottom and crafted staircases going up to the next level. We walked up to the next level and saw everyone we knew just hugging and telling everyone, "Hello" and "Great to see you!" I have always been awful with names. Everyone that came up to me was, "Hey, Maya." I just smiled and looked at them. I didn't know their names. I just said "Hey, there" or "Yea girl/boy." This one guy came up to me and just hugged me. I looked at Noel and whispered, "Who is this?" She just gave me an "I don't know" look. "You look great Maya," he said, with a sweet smile. "You do too," I said. "Remember when we had class freshmen year?" He asked. I was thinking like, damn, I barely remember senior year and you are going that far back. "Yea man," I said. He just kept on talking.

Noel walked away before I could grab her hand. She started to walk and felt someone grab at her hand. It was Donald. He quickly took her into an empty room and closed the door. "You look amazing Noel," he smiled. "Thank you," she quickly said. He walked closer to her and she did not move at all. He raised his hand to her face and gently touched it. Her eyes closed for a moment. "I want you in my life, Noel," Donald told her. Noel couldn't say anything. She was scared to love a man that hurt her friend, but could be the father of her baby. "I messed up everything," Noel expressed, with tears in her eyes. She saw a chair and walked over to it and sat down, because she felt light headed. "I know you've got a lot of decisions to make. I hope that one of them is allowing me to come into your life and heart," said Donald. He grabbed her hand and kneeled in front of her. Noel began to cry some more. "One day, I hope to do this with a ring in my hand. For now, I want to promise you that I love you, Noel, and this baby. I want to have a life and family with you. I can't change the past, but I will make sure to have a better future for the both of us." He leaned over and softly kissed Noel on the lips.

"Monica, I'm going to the lady's room. I will be right back," said Kim. As she was walking, she walked into a door she thought was the restroom and saw two people in there. Once she focused in, she recognized it was Noel and Donald. She wondered why Donald was kneeling in front of Noel, and then she saw them kiss. Kim's stomach dropped. She could not believe that her best friend and ex were kissing. Kim did not want to make a scene, so she quietly walked away. She finally found the restroom and went into one of the stalls. She began to cry. She was hurt and confused. She knew she was over Donald, but to see Noel kissing him was just too much! Then she got a text from Larry, "I love you so much, la flor." Kim realized that she has a wonderful man in her life right now. She wiped her tears and had to try to forget what she saw. As Kim walked to the sink, I came into the lady's room. I looked at Kim and said, "Are you alright?" Kim's response was, "I had something in my eye." She quickly walked out of the lady's room and I didn't give it another thought. Kim walked around and saw Donald and Noel come out of the room. Kim rushes up to her and ask, "Are you ok, Noel?" Noel was surprised and said, "Yes, I'm fine." Kim looked at Donald and said, "You are some piece of work." Kim

walked away to find Monica. They both looked puzzled, but parted ways.

Kim came up to Monica and grabbed the drink out of her hand and

swallowed it down quickly. Monica just looked at her, because Kim was

not a drinker. It took Monica a while to get the drink in the first place,

because of the long line at the bar. "I saw something I could not believe,

Monica," said Kim. She looked around and quietly said, "I saw Donald

kiss Noel." Monica had to play it off, since she already knew. "What! Are

you serious?" said Monica. Kim shook her head, "Yes." Monica was kind

of surprised to see how calm Kim was. Monica cautiously asked her,

"How do you feel about it?" Kim said, "I am pissed off at Noel and

Donald, but I'm not going to say anything." Monica did a sigh of relief

until Kim said, "When they least expect it, expect It.!" Monica said, "Oh

Damn." I was walking around when I saw Ethan walking towards me. I

smoothly tried to check to see if everything was right on me before he

approached. "Maya, you're fine as always," he smiled. I just smiled,

because I know it to be true. "So, we are still on for the midnight love thing," he smirked. I wanted him to take me now, but I knew deep down, I need to see where his mind was, because again, homecoming seemed to always be the one weekend hook ups. I told him, "Yes, I will see you later." He walked away, but I noticed something weird. He had a lipstick stain on his cheek. I didn't say anything because a lot of the time, different people come up and hug and kiss you if they haven't seen you for a while. It wasn't my place, since he wasn't my man. So, I kept on walking. I came up to Monica and Kim. The look that Monica had on her face was between "OMG" and "Hell to the no!" "Maya, I saw Noel and Donald kissing in a closed room," Kim expressed in one breath. I was pissed that Noel did that so I did not have to act surprised, because I was more shocked than anything. Yes, Noel did it this time! However, I was surprised that Kim was calm. "I can't believe that Donald would stoop down so low to force himself on Noel." I gave a puzzled look to Monica. "Noel has been through so much," said Kim. OMG! Kim thinks that Donald is taking advantage of Noel because of John. Monica's mouth dropped to her ankles. "Excuse us Kim, I need Maya to show me where the restroom is,"

Monica yelled out, as she grabbed me and rushed us to the restroom. "I can't believe this. This is some bullshit," Monica said. "Maya, I know Kim is not that blind," as she walked back and forth. The ladies in the restroom were starting to eavesdrop, so we headed to the lounge area and sat down. I said to Monica, "The mess is going to hit the fan, once Kim knows the entire truth. I am not going to volunteer myself to tell her either. That is Noel's job." We both sat there for a moment, just trying to stay away from the mess that could destroy our friendship. "Well, the first thing I am going to do is find Donald and kick his ass," I told Monica. Monica said, "Leave a cheek for me."

We both walked out of the restroom and saw Donald. We walked up to him like some pimps about to smack a worker for not getting his or her money. "Ladies," Donald said. I grabbed his arm and pinched it like a child about to get it for being bad. Monica had his other arm and we quickly walked him to another room. Monica pushed him on purpose, while I made sure to lock the door behind us. "Sit your ass down!" Monica ordered. He tried to act hard, but she jumped up like she was going to hit him and he quickly sat down. I walked over to him like a cop interrogating a criminal together in a locked room. I came out and said, "Kim saw you kiss Noel tonight." He looked down and said, "Yes, I did." "In all the places, why would you do it here and tonight? Hell, you could have done it when you got back to the hotel," I told him. Monica was the look out to make sure that no one was trying to come into the room. However, she would yell over to him, "Dumb-ass!" "Donald, it seems that you love Noel, but you had an 8-year relationship with Kim. You are selfish and are about to help destroy a friendship. Monica yelled, "Stupid ass!" Donald looked up and said, "I have always loved Noel. I am sorry that you see me as a monster, but I will be with her and my baby. "I can't take this crap anymore," said Monica. She charged over to Donald and got right up in his face. "Listen to me, Donald, I don't care if you are Romeo and Noel is Juliet, you fucked up. You could not get it right the first time, so you are trying to take dry Playdoh and rewet it. Do you know what it makes, a hot mess! If you love Noel like you say, then you need to make her come clean about the entire relationship. If you don't, you will be living a lie

156

and be lying to people about the lie to get by. So man up, and tell Kim the truth." Monica walked away. I turned to Donald and said, "And that is all I have to say, too." Donald got up quickly and hurried out of the room. I turned to Monica and asked, "Monica, where did you get all that from?" "Honey, when you have three kids, you become the lawyer and the judge!" She walked out of the room and all I could do was follow her. I was tired of all the crap that was going on tonight. Kim seeing Noel kissing Donald! What else can go wrong?

"Hello, Maya," said the crazy girl from college. I called her crazy because she tried to get the girls' attention by doing crazy things. I remember she came into my room and told us that she didn't like sex. So Monica said, "So why do you screw a lot of guys, then?" Honestly, all I could do is just look at her, as well. She wasn't all there. "So you look good," she smirked. I just looked at her. I don't have time for short talk or any type of conversation. "I'm fine," I made myself say. "Well, I am doing great. I am engaged to Greg from school," she forced her hand in my face to show me the ring with the chipped, diamond-like stone. I didn't want to laugh, so I said, "Oh, its dainty." She quickly pulled it back and said, "Greg is with

our twins, so I could come out and represent us." I thought to myself that

he must not care about his image. "Well, one day you will be as happy as I

am," she smiled. I looked at her and said, "I'm happy, because I know the

man I will have won't be anyone's second choice. At least the ring my ex

gave me was big enough to see. Have a good night." She was speechless

and I just walked off with the biggest smile on my face.

Chapter Twelve

No More, Please

Two hours in, I finally was able to mingle some more. I was able to dance and even get a free drink. I was finally having a good time. Monica was relaxing and talking with Sandra. Kim was mostly on the phone with Larry and Noel was nowhere to be seen. Fun was back in play, until Kim came up to me and said, "I can't find Noel." I asked Kim, "Have you texted her?" Kim said with a worried face, "Yes, but she's not responding. Can you text her?" I did not want to get in the middle of anything, but I did not want Kim to worry me to death, as well. Before I was about to text Noel, she beat me to the punch. Her text said, "I decided to leave with Donald, so we could talk some more. I did not want to take another chance of Kim finding us together. Tell everyone I'm ok and took a taxi back. Please, Maya, don't say anything!" I looked up at Kim's face and quickly say, "Noel was not feeling well, so she took a taxi back to the hotel." "Oh, we should be there for her, Maya," expressed Kim. Honestly, I couldn't take anymore of Kim babying Noel. I wanted to slap her to wake her up from the lies that Noel was not telling her. Plus, I felt like crap, because now I was deeper in the lie with Noel. Man, I need to find Monica, but she's probably getting a drink. I quickly left Kim where she was standing and headed towards the bar. "Bartender, I need a T and S on the rocks." He looked at me and said, "A what?" "Sorry, a Tequila and Sprite on the rocks, please," I gave a crazy smile. I was trying to get my head in order, when Monica walked up behind me. "So what is up, lady?" she said. I looked at her and said, "Noel left with Donald." The bartender gave me the drink and I tried to sip on it. "WTF!" Monica said. Monica's eyes rolled so far back in her head, I thought she was going to pass out. Monica said, "Is fool written on my forehead?" "Well, it's written on Kim's, because she seems blind in the matter," I said. The sad thing is that Kim is our friend and so is Noel. However, Noel's actions will be jeopardizing not just to her, but all of us since we know what's going on between her and Donald. "I have given up on Noel," Monica shouted. Monica yelled out to the bartender to get his attention when Sandra walked over. "What's up ladies?" Sandra asked. Monica said, "Kim is dumb and Noel is a dumb ass!" Sandra just looked at us and said, "Wow, I guess things are not getting any better with the get-a-long gang." "Girlfriend, you don't know the half of it," said Monica. From that moment, Monica realized that she just gave the universal sign of acceptance to her past lover, now friend. Monica looked like she just sucked on a lemon and Sandra just grinned from ear to ear. Well, I thought, as least we have a new friend just in case everything goes to pot with Kim or Noel. "Maya, I wanted to ask you a question," said Sandra. "Would you go to the restroom with me? I gave her a questionable look, but agreed to go. I asked Sandra, "Where have you been going to since you have been here?" She said that this was the first time she had to go tonight, but it was for something else. I was fine with it, since I have been going with everyone else. When we got into the restroom, she checked to see if anyone was in there. Sandra turned to me and said, "Cover me." I looked at her and asked, "Why?" She looked around and said, "Because I still got my dick." My eyes felt like they were

going to jump out of my head. I asked, "You didn't get an operation?" "I

did, but for these up here," as she grabbed her breasts. When it was time to

remove my dick, I freaked out and told the doctor I needed time to think

on it. "Maya, I'm partially completed," Sandra sadly expressed. I did not

know what to say. For all the TLC shows I have seen, I know it was

probably more of an ornament than anything. "There is no erection due to

the hormones I'm taking," she said. However, I have not learned to piss

sitting down. I saw the concern in her face. "Well, do like all women do at

public restrooms, squat over the toilet." Sandra's eyes lit up. "But you

have to piss standing above the toilet looking toward the door." She went

into the stall and pulled up her dress. I felt weird for two reasons. One, for

showing a man, now woman how to pee and second, showing a grown

man, now woman how to pee. I told Sandra, I'm going to close the door

and let you do your thing. "Don't go too far Maya," Sandra said. I heard

her heels tapping on the ground and soon relieved herself. "Yes! Yes!" she

said, very relieved. Some women were coming into the restroom with their

162

faces turned up. "She had an UTI," I said. They said, "Damn, those things

are the worst." As Sandra came out, one of the woman said, "Girl, I have

been there, cranberry juice is the key." Sandra looked at me puzzled and I

told her, "I will explain later." As we walked out of the restroom, I ran

face slapped into Ethan. "We seem to meet up in the strangest places," he

grinned at me. I did not know what to say but, "yes." He leaned over to

me and whispered in my ear, "Midnight is still a go to see your beautiful

face." All I could do is just smile and giggle. He walked away and Sandra

said, "He got your thong in a twist." I looked at her and just gave her a

slap on her arm. 11:30pm came, and I didn't know it was getting so late.

Since we drove up in two cars, thanks to Kim's man, I tried to text the

girls that I would be leaving soon. I saw Monica and told her that I would

be heading back to the hotel for my Midnight rendezvous. Monica just

looked at me and said, "Fine Heifer." I told her, "Don't hate because your

opportunity changed." She just rolled her eyes at me. However, I didn't

want to tell her that Sean's past passion meat was still there. Mostly it just

hung there for décor. I just laughed to myself and walked away. As I was going out the door, I ran into Kim. She was looking kind of out of it. As a woman that hasn't had a man in some months, I wanted to sprint to the car without her seeing me. However, as a friend, I walked by her hoping this situation could be solved very quickly. "Hey, Kim," I said. She acted jumpy as if she was not mentally there. Her eyes were empty and red, but she said, "Hey." I remembered this look. It was from the numerous times that Donald stood her up or we were at the clinic due to his whorish ways. I was concerned for Kim. She had a wonderful heart and the last thing she needs right now is an ex and a friend announcing their "love child." "Maya, I can't believe that Noel was kissing Donald," she whispered. I heard the hurt in her voice, not a confused type of hurt, but a pissed at them type of hurt. I couldn't say much because I did not want to open up the windows of conversation, but I did say, "Are you ok?" She looked up at me as if I just asked the dumbest question possible. "I should not be mad, especially with marrying Larry, but Noel is supposed to be my sister." "That Bitch is supposed to be my sister!" I just realized that Kim is past pissed. I was actually scared to say anything. I have never heard Kim call any women a Bitch, but I guess things can change. Kim looked up at me and asked, "So, do you think I should be mad?" That was a split answer for me. One side felt that Noel is wrong especially with me knowing more about the situation than Kim. However, one side felt that Kim has a wonderful future ahead with Larry. Shoot, he is fine, Latin and treats her like the queen that she deserves to be treated. But, I answered her, "I know it can be hard, but remember to never go backward when beauty is just ahead of you. Well, I have to go meet Ethan at the hotel. I will see you later," as I walked away. I love Kim, but she can become winded if I did not walk away.

As I approached the car, I saw something out of the corner of my eye. It was Ethan, and he was with the woman with the dainty engagement ring. I was going to turn around and speak, and then they began to kiss. I just stared and couldn't say anything. I felt used, but I was wondering how many women has he kissed this entire weekend? I quickly got into the car. I felt some kind of way. I didn't know how to feel since he wasn't my man. But, I was pissed because he took advantage of me. Damn, this single crap kills me! I just turned up the music and the wrong song came on, "All I really want is to be Happy." That was an ironic kick in the ass. I was still going to show up for our meeting. However, I was going to make sure this man understands that he cannot play with me. I drove up to the hotel and sat in the car for a minute. I wasn't going to rush to the bar like some desperate woman. I had a plan that needed to be executed well. When I looked up, I saw Ethan get out of the car and take something out of his pocket to wipe the lipstick off his lips. As I saw this, I knew what I was going to do. He entered the hotel and I began to get ready. I freshen up my makeup and popped a mint in my mouth. As I opened the door, I told myself, "Let the fun begin." I'm glad the hotel's doors opened up automatically. I thought to myself that my presence was so heavenly, due to harp music playing in my mind, until I realized there was a woman playing the harp in the lobby. As I approached the bar, I saw Ethan walking towards me. He was about to kiss me on the lips, but I quickly turn my head, so he was only able to kiss my cheek. I didn't want him to kiss me after seeing him lay face with another woman just a moment ago.

166

He said, "Baby, I wanted some sweet lip from you." I smiled and said, "Well, I ate something funky a few minutes ago and I didn't want you to experience it." He grabbed my hand and led me to the table that he was sitting at. He pulled out the chair and at once, I sat down. After he took his seat, I just looked at him. Playing over in my mind was the way he kissed me at the game and the person I saw him kiss prior to our meeting. "You look wonderful, Maya," he said with a devilish grin. "Thank you," I said. He waved to the bartender to get his attention. "Two drinks, please," Ethan shouted. I told him, "I'm ok." The bartender came and said, "It's nice to see you again." I just laughed. "So, the bartender knows you," said Ethan. "Well, I better be protective of my lady." Now, if it was the old Maya, I would have just melted. But, the new Maya knew this was a crock of shit. I couldn't believe that I was about to go through this crap again. However, the difference was that I did not have to go through four years of marriage to find out the man was an asshole. "Baby, why are you not drinking? Is something on your mind?" asked Ethan. "You know what, there is something on my mind," I told him. I began my story to him.

"Well, I saw a…Something is in my eye, do you have a tissue?" I asked. This fool pulled out the same handkerchief that he used to wipe off the lipstick. I put the evidence in his face and said, "And, that is what was on my mind!" I started to get up from the table and he grabbed my arm. Vincent came in and said, "Man, don't grab a woman like that." Ethan stepped back because Vincent was a built man and Ethan had a little girth on him. "Ethan, I enjoyed our moment, but it seems you enjoyed kissing the crazy girl who is engaged." Ethan looked at me and couldn't say anything and walked away. That was the last I saw of him. I was so mad at myself that I forgot that Vincent was even there. He just stood there and didn't say anything to me. I started to walk away till he grabbed my hand. "Would you join me for a drink, Maya," he asked. One part of me wanted to just go to my room, but I said, "Yes." He pulled out the chair at the bar and told the bartender to bring two waters and a menu for us. I actually begin to perk up because a sister was getting hungry. "So Maya, why is a beautiful woman like you by yourself?" he asked. Now, I did not want to jump crazy and say the wrong thing, so I asked him what he meant by this question. He looked at me and laughed. He said, "I meant to say it's not safe for you to be by yourself, but also you would be a blessing to a man." He sounded so good with everything he said, especially with his accent. We talked and laughed that I forgot about the time. He told me that he was visiting because he was getting ready for his cousin's wedding. He was single and was preparing himself for that special woman whenever she comes. I told him about my past and he was surprised at how my marriage ended. He called my ex-husband an "el Gilipollas." I laughed. We talked until I realized it was 2am. "It was a pleasure to be in your presence, Maya," he said as he kissed my hand. I smiled and I got up from the bar. He quickly turned to me and asked, "May I walk you to your room?" "Yes, please," I smiled. He got up and we walked through the lobby to the elevator. I wanted him to kiss me, but I kind of felt like it was too soon and we were going to be in Kim's wedding. Plus, if something happened and it didn't work out, it would be awful. He looked at me and asked, "Are you ok, you look like you are thinking hard." I just smiled. Darn, I never could control my facial expressions. As the doors opened, he held out his arm and I put my arm around his. We had some small talk till we got to my room. "It was a pleasure to be with you, Maya," Vincent said, as he kissed my hand. "Thank you and with you, as well," I said. Then, he walked away. I opened the door and saw Monica sitting up in the bed as if she was waiting for me. I had a smile tattooed on my face. "So, how was Ethan?" she asked. "It was amazing," I grinned. "Girl, I saw you with Vincent! You know my ass is nosy," Monica laughed. I just fell on the bed with the biggest grin. I could not say anything, because I was trying to replay it in my mind. "Earth to Maya," Monica snapped at me. "What?" I said with a confused look. Monica rolled her eyes again at me and said, "Tell me about you and Vincent." Well, I gave her a quick overview on how I saw Ethan kissing the crazy girl from school in the parking lot. The sad thing is she is supposed to be engaged like her fake-ass said. Monica was just taking it all in and then I said, "Then, Vincent came in and saved me. Then, Ethan grabbed my arm in a crazy way." Monica looked and said, "It seems that this could be the start of something special or not." I looked at Monica. I hate when she is straight to the point. Yes, in my mind there could be something possible, but he is just visiting. I cannot start thinking of any relationship for the future. Then, I heard a knock on the door. I got up from the bed and looked through the peephole. It was Vincent. I quickly ran over to Monica for her to check my face to make sure that everything was still the same. I ran back to the door and opened it with much grace. "Hello Vincent, May I ask what brought you back?" I said, with a half-ass seductive voice. "I forgot to give you something," he smiled. In my head, I don't remember dropping anything. So I looked up at him confused, until he leaned over with the door wide open and kissed me on the lips. Monica was jumping on the bed, looking crazy and smiling. All I could do was just take it all in. "Good Night, Maya," he smoothly said, as he walked away. I felt something in my stomach that I haven't felt in a while. Also, somewhere else in the lower region finally got an early morning wakeup call. I closed the door and performed the craziest dance in front of Monica. Monica got up and joined me as well.

We were celebrating till I saw the joining door from the other room open. "Have you seen Kim?" Noel asked me with the saddest face. "Remember,

Kim said she would be staying with Larry," I told her. Noel just had a

blank look on her face. Monica gave me a look that signaled me to get rid

of Noel because she didn't want to hear her problems with Donald again.

"Well, Noel……" I tried to get out. She quickly falls on the bed and

Monica darted into the bathroom to avoid the conversation. DAMN! I

rolled my eyes and sat on the bed. "Maya, I think that I'm going to tell

Kim tomorrow about the entire situation. "Ok," I quickly said and got off

the bed. Noel would always pull the "stop me" mode on us, but we are not

in college anymore. Life is crazy enough to bring more drama to the table.

"So, I should go and destroy my friendship by telling her the truth," Noel

stuttered. I just looked at her and said, "You did that the day you allowed

Donald in your bed. Noel stormed out the room and slammed the door.

Monica peeked out of the door as waiting for the coast to be clear. "Man, I

really had to go to the bathroom," she laughed. I just glared at her and got

ready for bed.

Chapter Thirteen

Weeping at Night: Joy at Daylight?

"Baby, what is wrong," asked Larry as he was massaging Kim's back. Kim knew that she could not tell her new man that she was pissed to see her old man kissing her friend. She had to tell him without making it seem like it was her. "Baby, there was a situation I saw that kind of got to me," she said. He got up and sat right in front of her to give his undivided attention. "Well, a girl from school told me that she saw one of her ex's kissing one of her friends. The girl was confused because she was pissed as hell to see it, but she is in a wonderful relationship and didn't know why," Kim explained. Larry looked at her for a moment and said, "Well, it would be painful to see your friend kissing a past lover because you would question why her and not me," he said. Kim looked at Larry and he leaned over and kissed her tenderly. "Kim, the past is what it is.

173

You need to tell the friend that if she is happy, she needs to let it go. It's not going to be easy, but she cannot love now what was then," Larry said in loving words. Kim was still pissed and confused at the answer Larry gave her, but what else could she do. Donald was her first in everything. She always felt robbed after giving her body to Donald and that's why she's waiting to make love to Larry. She knows what sex and screwing is, but she wants more now. "Baby, I want you to be happy because you deserve to be," he smiled and gently kissed her forehand. He knew she had something on her mind and he wanted to make sure to get it out. He looked into her eyes and said, "I can't make love to you yet, but I will kiss your lips tonight." Kim got up and was able to kiss him. He backed up and stated, "The ones that are hidden from me. I want to relax you." He picked her up and laid her across the bed. He started kissing her and slowly undressed her like a mother would undress her baby. She was cool and freaking out at the same time. He took his strong arms and spread her legs apart. Kim started to drift off to a state of euphoria. She never felt tenderness the way that Larry was giving her. She couldn't speak, but

174

thought about what she wanted to say. Her body was like a time bomb

about to explode with passion and confusion. As she reached her peak, a

single tear came from her eye because she didn't want others to hear her

outburst. Larry got up and went to the sink to wipe his mouth and brought

a towel over for Kim to dry herself off. "How are you, baby?" he grinned.

She looked into his eyes and said, "Relaxed." He wiped her down and

climbed on top of her. He took his hand and moved her hair from her face.

"I love you so much, baby. I can't wait to make love to my bride," he said.

Kim looked into his eyes and said, "I love you, too." He got off of her and

prepared himself for bed. Kim wanted to take a shower and walked into

the bathroom. As she turned on the shower, so did her tears. She was

confused because she was with a wonderful man that just satisfied her, but

is crying over what she saw between Noel and Donald.

As I lay in bed, Vincent's kiss just played over and over in my head. His

lips were so soft and I tingled so hard when he did it. I was about to drift

off to sleep till Monica said, "So what do you think about Noel telling

Kim?" At first, I did not want to answer and play like I was asleep. "Maya,

I know you are still awake, just answer the question," snapped Monica. I turned around and said, "Well, I really don't know what is going to happen since the wedding is over 10 months away. I do know that Noel will probably have the baby by then depending on how far along she is." A look came across Monica's face as if something scared her. "You're right. She could be 2 or 3 months pregnant, now. The baby would be here by April or May," she explained. I just looked over at her, because I really wanted to go to sleep. I was tired and needed to dream about my kiss with Vincent. "Good night," yawned Monica. I turned over and closed my eyes. I was going to milk that kiss in my dreams as much as I could.

In the morning, we all were in dreamland. The only thing that got me up was I had to go to the bathroom. As I stumbled through the room, I thought I heard voices in Noel's room. I was too sleepy to care so I thought it was nothing. As I passed back by the door, I heard moaning and laughing. I can't believe that Noel was in the room with Donald. I looked at the clock and it was 6:30am. I knew I was wrong for thinking this, but I didn't care. I quietly put on my shoes and tip toed to the door to leave the room. I was always good at impersonating Kim, so I took my room key and started to put it in the door. "Noel, why can't I get in the door, my key is not working," I said, while trying not to laugh. I heard rushing and crashing in the room. "Wait Kim, I'm coming," shouted Noel. After opening the door, she turned and looked at me. "Maya, you scared the hell out of me," she said. "Why is Donald in the room with you," as I walked into the room. "No Maya," as she was pushing me out of the room. I was walking toward the bathroom and opened the door. I thought my eyes were going to pop out of my head. "Hey, Maya," said John, standing there with a sheet wrapped around himself. I turned to Noel after closing the door. I said, "Noel, you are pregnant by Donald and you are screwing John, who is about to get married next weekend. What in the hell is wrong with you?" "I am so confused," said Noel. "That's bullshit. You're just a selfish bitch," I shouted. I couldn't be in the room with her anymore. I was so pissed. I went back over to the room and quietly slammed the door. I got into bed and heard Monica ask, "What happened?" I wanted to go back to sleep, since I had to drive back later, so I lied. "Nothing, caught

Noel and Donald doing something," I joked with her. "Heifer, don't you lie to me. I heard everything from the door," Monica said. "I don't want to talk about it, Monica," I pleaded with her. "I just can't believe you called her a bitch," she laughed. I just turned in the bed away from Monica's face and rolled my eyes. I didn't like what I said because I don't like to down any women. Women should support each other. However, Noel showed me a side that I couldn't understand. First, she gets pregnant by our best friend's ex and now was caught trying to sleep with her ex that is about to get married. I was more pissed about John, because she could try to frame him by saying they had sex at homecoming and that this could be his baby. That's some crazy shit. "Maya, we are knowingly involved in a dumb love triangle," said Monica. I turned over and told her, "The hell I am!" Monica gets up and says, "You know that we know about Noel and Donald and now John. We have to be careful because Noel has fuel and could tell Kim and play it against us as if we knew everything." Monica does make sense. Noel is my friend, but she's so emotional and could try to play the "they knew too" card. "We definitely have to talk with Noel later and see how we or Noel is going to tell Kim."

After that, I went back to sleep. As I started to dream, I saw Ethan coming toward me in a field of flowers. He started running to me and I just stood there. As he ran, his facial expression changed. He stopped and looked like something scared the crap out of him and he turned the other way. As I looked behind me, it was Vincent with his shirt off and he was well-oiled all over his chest. He walked up to me and he grabbed my waist. I looked into his eyes and he gently touched my face. He smiled and said, "Get up Maya." Monica was hovering over me. "Damn," I said. There was a knock on the door and Sandra came in. "Rise and shine, beauties," she said. "I told Sean, I mean, Sandra to come because he has always been good at helping us with problems," said Monica. "I need some coffee, so I called room service," said Sandra. I was trying to close my eyes to get that dream back, but it was gone. I sat up on the bed and rubbed my eyes. I just said, "So what is the plan." There was a knock on the door and a voice saying, "Room service." Sandra walked over and opened the door. The waiter came into the room with a table with coffee, fresh fruit, croissants and anything else you could think of. "Charge it to room 222," she said as she tipped the waiter. "Thank you for breakfast, Sandra," I said. She looked at me while sipping her coffee, "Don't thank me. Thank James because the room service is on his card. I'm learning." Monica couldn't say anything, but cheered with Sandra by hitting her coffee mug with Sandra's. "So, I heard from Monica what happened. WTF is wrong with Noel? She was always the smart one, but I think it must be book smarts because common sense is not one of her strong point." All that Monica and I could do was laugh because Sandra was telling the truth. I reminded both of them to be a little quieter since she could be hearing our conversation right now. Monica always gets loud when she's excited over every little thing. "I don't care what Noel says to me. You know I will read her down," Monica shouted. I said, "Calm your ass down, Monica." "Monica, are you auditioning for something because we have enough drama going on right now," snapped Sandra. I giggled to myself while Monica got quiet. "Noel

180

is our friend and she needs our help or some help, but help is needed," said Sandra. Both Monica and I agreed with Sandra.

All I know is in a few hours we will be going back to our lives and Kim and Noel's friendship could end. Before we got into a deep discussion, there was a knock at the door. I guess it was my turn to get up and answer the door. I looked through the peephole and it was Noel. "It's Noel," I whispered. They both looked at me with wide eyes, but I knew I had to answer the door. Noel walked into the room looking like a hot mess. I don't know if it was from lack of sleep or crying, but she looked awful. She didn't say anything. She just walked over to the chair and plopped down on it. "Good morning, Sunshine," said Sandra. "I don't feel like joking around right now," she mocked. Sandra kept sipping on her coffee and giggling in the cup. "So, I guess you all know about what happened this morning. No one in here is a Saint. We all have done something in our lives that we regret. Don't judge me," Noel yelled. We all just stared at her because she has lost it. The room was quiet for a moment. Sandra put down her cup and said, "Well, I cannot judge you for your dumb actions.

However, Noel, you are more than this. What is truly going on with you? This is a "What would Jesus do" moment and it's looking like you are on your own." "This feels like an intervention with no drugs, alcohol or food involved, but you are just a friend making dumb ass decisions," said Monica. "We all love you Noel. We are not trying to lessen your worth because you are doing a great job on your own." Noel just started crying like someone just hit her in the face. She started shaking because of the pain inside. The tears were falling like rain and the only thing we all could do was just look at her. I got up and grabbed her. I just held her. She collapsed on me like a tired baby. It hurts me to see Noel like this. Even the strongest woman can be weak. The world is no joke on the strong. "Maya, I'm scared and I don't want to end up like my mom." I knew Noel's backstory which was her biggest fear. I wiped her face with the tissues next to the bed. "You are not your parents," I said. I explained to Noel, "You are successful and well off, but your worth is not in your bank account. It's what you see in the mirror. It's what your soul feels when you smile with your heart. Only you can feel it." I said, "I remember when

I was leaving my ex-husband, He told me that I would never have a man as good as he was, and I said, Thank God! I tell you this because love is from God and yourself. Judgment cannot come from anyone but you. However, you have to stop this, because not only will you lose your friends, you could lose yourself in the process." Noel looked at us. She was speechless. Sandra got up off the bed and came over to Noel. She looked at her and said, "You have to accept you for you, baby girl. We are here for you." Sandra hugged Noel for a long time. Even Monica came and hugged her too. "Thank you guys. This means the world to me that you are here," said Noel. She wiped her eyes and walked to the door. As she turned, she said, "The only fear is that I may lose my sister. Then, Noel walked out of the room. We all looked at each other as if we had accomplished this great task, but deep down we knew that this was only the beginning.

Chapter Fourteen

Time to Go

Kim woke up in Larry's arms. She realized that this was not a dream and he was real. She always felt that the relationship with Larry was a dream, but it was truly her reality. "Good morning, baby." He gently kisses her on the cheek. She looked at him and smiled. He gets out of the bed and walks to the bathroom. "So, I will be staying two more days because I have business meetings this week, baby. Would you like to stay with me?" he asked. Kim didn't have to go back to work until Tuesday, but she didn't want to be tempted, as well. She said, "I better be heading back since I have a lot to do on Monday, but I can change my ticket for a later flight." He poked his head out of the bathroom and said, "I would like that because I can spend more time with you." Kim was getting her phone and realized that she would need to take Noel to the airport since they rode in together. "Baby, I have to take Noel to the airport," said Kim. She didn't know if he heard her, so she walked to the door. She noticed that Larry was staring in the mirror. "Baby, are you ok?" Kim asked. He quickly looked at her and said, "Yes baby, I'm fine." Kim said, "I just wanted to tell you that I have to drop Noel off at the airport since we came in together." Larry smiled and said, "Ok." Kim was concerned about Larry because recently, he would be there and then be out of it. She didn't want to think that anything was wrong with him, but her intuition was starting to get to her. "Baby, you would tell me if something was wrong?" she asked. He looked at her and said, "Of course." They hugged, but Larry's faced changed as if something was over his head. "I'm going to get in the shower and get myself ready for you," he said. She smiled and gave him a kiss and left. She walked out of the bathroom and he sat down on the toilet. He thought to himself, "I just lie to the woman I loved." Kim wanted to get ready herself, so she wrote a note and left it on the bed. She walked out of the room with a song in her heart. She knew that in less than a year, she was going to be married to the man of her dreams. She was so happy.

As she walked to the room, she saw Donald. He was walking straight in her direction. He stopped right in front of her. "I have to tell you something, Kim," he said. Kim didn't say anything. "I want you know that I apologize for everything I have said or done to you. I was an asshole and I take full responsibility on my part," Donald explained. He continued by saying, " I said this because I will soon be a father and found the love of my life, just like you have in that guy you're about to marry. I don't want there to be any hard feelings, since you know the woman. I hope that we all can be friends." Kim said, "I am happy for you and whoever you are with. Yes, you did hurt me very much, but I had to forgive you." They both smiled. Donald said, "I am happy because the woman is Noel." In an instance, Kim's demeanor changed. "You said the woman is Noel?" Kim said. Kim kicked Donald right in the balls. He fell to the ground with a big thud. "You asshole, you could have liked any other woman, but you go and screw my friend. I take back what I said to you. So, you are the father of her baby, too? I should kick your ass right now." She kicked him again,

but in the leg. Donald was in so much pain that he couldn't say anything,

but just lay still and hope she wouldn't kick him anymore. "You know, I

am happy that I don't have to deal with an asshole like you anymore!

Larry is a good man and knows how to treat a woman, you asshole!"

shouted Kim. As Sandra opened the door, Kim stood right there. Kim

stormed into the room and Sandra looked down at Donald holding himself.

Sandra just shook her head and said in a deep voice, "Man, that little

woman just kicked your ass." All Donald could do is look up and agree

with Sandra. She came in the room, crying and pissed off. "What is

wrong?" asked Sandra. Kim just fell on my bed. Kim said, "Donald just

told me that Noel was the woman he was in love with." All of us did not

say a word. We all knew that if we told her the truth about the entire

weekend, she would go off. So Monica, the actress said, "No!" Sandra

gave a look like she was right to get the hell out of this room, but she

walked over to the chair and sat down. I felt like this entire weekend was a

soap opera. At this point, I was ready to go home. I was tired from all of this crap. The only thing that was wonderful the entire weekend was Vincent's kiss. Man, I was milking it as much as I could. I asked, "Kim, how do you feel about this?" Kim looked at me and said, "I don't know. I am pissed, but I have a great man now. I can't believe that Noel kept this from me. I thought she was my sister." Kim was hurt. Not only did Noel lie, she felt betrayed as well. "Well, I am not going to say anything to her about it," said Kim. At the same time, Monica and Sandra said, "What?" "If Noel is my friend, she will come clean and tell me the truth. If she doesn't, I know the bitch is a liar." I made an expression on my face that said, "Damn" with Kim saying that word about Noel. I thought to myself that we all are guilty for knowing the truth about Noel and Donald. How is she going to treat us because we are all as wrong as Noel for keeping the truth from her? All of us are guilty. "Well, I have to take Noel to the airport, because I am taking a later flight to spend some more time with Larry. I hope she will talk to me during the ride there." Sandra shouted, "Well, it was good seeing you all and I got to go. See you all at the wedding." She quickly left the room. I bet Sandra was walking back to her room, thanking God that she was out of the room.

Once Sandra left the room, there was a knock on the door of the joining room. Monica went to open the door and it was Noel, acting happy. "Good morning everyone, It's a beautiful day," said Noel. We all looked at her like something was off, but we just kept it to ourselves. "I can't believe that this is it. The next time we see each other will be at Kim's wedding," she smiled. Monica gave me a look like Noel must have snapped. I just looked back at Kim because she wants to know the truth, but I don't think that Noel was even going to go down that road. "Well, we should all get ready and find somewhere we can have lunch before we part. Kim said, "Yes, we do need to decide where, since I have to take you to the airport, Noel." Kim looked spaced out. I know that she was pissed, but wanted to know the God-honest truth because she would go off on Noel. This situation could destroy our friendship or just make us stronger as sisters. "I guess I will see you two ladies in a minute," said Kim to Monica and me.

They walked into the room and Noel closed the door. "Something wicked this way comes," laughed Monica. All I could do was just roll my eyes.

"So, how was it last night with your man," asked Noel. Kim just looked at Noel and said, "It was nice." Kim really didn't want to say anything to her. Noel came over to Kim and touched her shoulder and said, "Girlfriend is everything ok?" Kim looked at her and deep down; she wanted to punch Noel in the mouth. However, Kim said, "I'm ok." Kim quickly ran into the bathroom and closed the door. She collapsed on the toilet and began to cry with the water running so Noel wouldn't hear her. Noel just felt sick. She didn't know if it was the baby or the betrayal to her sister. Noel just fell on the bed and began to cry. Monica had her ear to the door and said, "Sounds like someone is crying." I just looked up at her. I had nothing else to say. All I knew is that in a few months, there was going to be a wedding and a baby. There were a lot of things to plan out, but I didn't want to neglect Noel. "I guess we need to have a baby shower for her," I said. Monica looked at me and just rolled her eyes. "Maya, don't you feel some kind of way with what Noel did to Kim?" questioned Monica. I said,

"What can we do? I can't take sides because they are both our sisters. I just don't want us to pick a side and go against each other." That was how I felt about it. Situations like this can tear friendships apart. Monica got up off the bed to take a shower and she said, "Well, all I can promise is I will stay out of the mess as much as I can." I gave a grin and she went into the bathroom. I just sat there wondering if this was really happening now or was it just a dream. I was praying that some person would appear and say; "Gotcha." There was a knock at the door. God answers prayers, I thought. As I walked to the door and opened it, it was Donald. "Damn," I said. "Maya, I have to talk with you, please," he asked. Looking at him, he looks like he was in pain. I asked, "Are you ok?" "It's a long story," he said. I ran to the bathroom and quickly told Monica, I would be back. She couldn't even get a word in which was fine with me. I would tell her later. I quickly left the room because I didn't want Kim or Noel to hear this conversation. "Please come to my room," he pleaded. "Ok, I will, but if you try something or say something wrong, I'm gone," I said. He didn't say a word, but just shook his head. I quickly followed him to his room and sat in the chair, but I didn't know what he could have done in the bed. He slowly limped to the bed and sat down. "I told Kim about me and Noel," as he looked at the floor. "What the F....! What is wrong with you and Noel! This was supposed to come out later like when homecoming was over," I yelled. He groaned. I mentioned, "I guess that is why you are in pain, because Kim kicked you in the balls!" All he could do was grin. I saw the bucket of ice and wrapped some ice in a towel and handed it to him. I felt bad because it probably hurt, but he deserved it. The sad thing is that Noel did it again by almost sleeping with John, I think. Donald seems to love Noel, but how can she love anyone else if she can't get right herself. He adjusted and said, "Maya, I know I was wrong in what I did to Kim now and years ago. I didn't know love. Kim was a wonderful girl. She loved me beyond myself, but I was selfish and self-center." He continued, "If it wasn't for meeting Noel and she telling me off; I probably would've never fell in love with her." "What did you say? You're in love with Noel," I questioned. He got up off the bed and somewhat walked over to the closet. He came back with a tiny box and opened it up. There was a big diamond engagement ring, shining like a star. I gave him a crazy look and asked, "So, what is this?" Donald smiled and said, "This is my grandmother's ring and I was going to give it to Noel for her hand in marriage." All I could do was think about how I just saw John wrapped in a sheet some hours ago and now seeing the man I grew to hate, kneeling in pain to show me his love for Noel. What the hell is wrong with Noel? "Maya, do you think Noel would marry me?" he asked. All I could say was, "You won't know till you ask." I quickly got up and walked toward the door. I wanted to tell him about what I saw, but I felt that it was not my place. All I could tell him, once I opened the door was, "Just be careful." I let the door close behind me, but it sounded like a loaded gun shot, due to all the guilt I had for Kim and Donald. I didn't want to get involved in their mess. I had enough of my own crap in my life. The only person I truly felt bad for was Kim. Kim is my sister and I hate that I have this secret hidden from her. I wondered if Kim knew the situation. And if so, does Noel know that Kim knows. OMG! I wonder what Kim is going to do to Noel? I rushed back to the room and opened the door. I shouted to Monica, but Kim was sitting on the bed. "Kim," I said, trying to play it off. She said, "Yes?" "Hey girl, I was just thinking about you aloud," I said in a joking manner. "Maya, you are so crazy," she laughed. I joined in and we were laughing together. I agreed with her by saying, "Yes, I am." "Well, I came in to tell you that I won't be able to join you girls for our yearly lunch before we all part. Since I have to take Noel to the airport, I wanted to have a private lunch with her. I hope you both understand," she expressed in a calm voice. Monica and I both drew a blank, till I spoke up and said, "We understand, Kim." All that Monica could do is just nod her head and smile. "Good, well, I will come back ladies afterward, so I can give you all a proper goodbye. We both just stood there and smiled and said, "Ok."

As she walked out of the room and closed the door, I took Monica's hand and pulled her into the bathroom. "Kim looked scary calm to me," Monica said. "She knows about Donald and Noel," I told Monica. Monica looked up and said, "So Donald told her about everything?" "Honestly, I don't truly know, but he got kicked in the balls, so I'm guessing he did. Monica

194

was quiet. Then she asked, "Was that the reason why you left in a hurry to talk to him?" I looked at her and nodded. "Plus, he showed me the ring he wants to give Noel for marriage." Monica gave a WTF look with her mouth wide open. "What in the hell is wrong with them! I understand my situation, until I realized the guy I wanted to screw is a woman now, but they are dumb as hell," she whispered. I felt it wasn't the time to tell Monica that Sandra still has his tool, but it was out of use. "Well, Monica, It's not about you right now. I wonder if we need to tell Noel about the situation," I said. Monica walked toward the bathroom and quickly turned around and said, "I'm not that self-centered, Maya. I care about the girls, but this crap is crazy." Then she closed the door. I actually agree with her about the craziness in this soap opera-type drama. I didn't want to draw attention by knocking on the door, because I didn't know if Kim was in the room. I looked on the table and saw my cell phone. I reached for it and saw a lot of text messages from Ethan, but I deleted them because I don't have time. Then, I saw a number I didn't recognize. I opened the text and it was from Vincent. He said, "I truly enjoyed your company last night and maybe we can keep in touch. Take care." Man! I did a little dance because

I was happy. Vincent is fine and I have no problem staying in touch with

him. After seeing that, I felt like I have a chance at getting back into the

dating game, even though, I can't stand it. Once you have been married,

dating is like renting from the video store. You have seen all of the movies

before, but you act like it's all new to you. I didn't want to become the

bitter woman, but I have to be willing to keep my heart open. Jesus would

have to come from Heaven on a cloud descending and point to him, and

say, "He is the one," and ascend back up to heaven before I believe it. I

know it's asking for the impossible, but after my ex, I'm willing to believe

in miracles. I started to look for Noel's number. Once I got her number, I

sent this message; Call me. I didn't want to say anything extra because

Kim is nosy and I didn't want her to think I knew about everything.

Hopefully, this too will pass.

There was a deep silence in Kim and Noel's room. No one dared to

speak a word, but they knew it had to be done. Kim's thoughts were on

Donald telling her about his love for Noel, her confusion since she was getting married and being pissed at Noel for sleeping with Donald. Noel

was scared as hell. She didn't even want to breathe loud for the fear of

Kim going off. Noel knew that Kim had a two-sided personality. One side

was about love and peace, while the other side was crazy as hell. I wish

she had a happy middle, but that's wishful thinking. Noel was packing and

felt a little sick, but continued to move forward. She didn't know if it came

from the deceit she felt or the new life growing inside. However, both

were growing inside her. Kim was also gathering the rest of her things to

take to Larry's room. She was confused herself with true love and past

pain. She could not believe that Donald betrayed her. She gave him so

much of her soul, life and body. Even the life that they would have had

together did not mean anything because he felt it would have kept him

back. Kim's mind was brewing over so many things. She was pissed at

Donald and Noel for their new love. However, she had Larry. It felt like a

double edge sword about the hate and love she is experiencing right now.

Kim asked Noel "So, when does your flight leave?" Noel was surprised.

She looked up and said, "At noon." "I wanted us to go to brunch," said

Kim. Noel quickly replied with, "I want to get to the airport as early as possible. I already called for a cab to come get me." Kim felt like she wanted to yell at Noel because this would be the chance to find out the truth about Donald. "Ok," said Kim. Noel was relieved in her head because she wouldn't have to face Kim with the fact that she was lying behind her back. Noel knocked on the door and I opened it. "Maya and Monica, I am heading to the airport early. I got a cab and I will be heading out in a few minutes," said Noel. I gave her a big hug and whispered in her ear, "Tell me when you want to have your baby shower and I will hook you up." Noel said, "I will and I will definitely be ready for Kim's wedding if I will still be invited, after everything." I wanted to tell her so badly that Kim knew about the entire situation, but it was not my place. I just smiled. "Come here, bitch," said Monica. Monica grabbed her and said, "Don't forget what we told you." Noel smiled and walked back into the room. Kim saw Noel come back into the room and Kim said, "At least let me help you to the front of the hotel." Noel was silent and said, "Ok." Noel was trying to move as fast as she could to get the hell out of that room. They both quickly left the room. The walk to the elevator felt like an eternity for both of them. The door opened and they walked in. Noel said, "I enjoyed seeing you." Kim said, "Me too." They walked out and got to the front of the hotel, where the cab was waiting for her. The driver quickly grabbed the bags and put them in the car. "Well, I will see you at your wedding, Kim," smiled Noel. Kim just stared at her and smoothly said, "Yes." The driver opened the door for Noel and she quickly got into the cab, trying to avoid looking at Kim. Kim closed the door and waved to her. As the cab pulled away, Kim said softly, "I know, bitch." Noel felt a sigh of relief and looked down at her phone. She noticed she had a text message waiting for her. It's from Donald. It said, "I love you with all my heart and I can't wait to see you at the airport, baby." She let out a grin then her phone started to ring. It's from me. "Hi Maya," she said. "Did Kim talk to you?" I asked. Noel seemed confused. "About what, Maya?" she giggled. I told Noel, "Kim knows everything!" The phone went silent.

About the Author

Natalie R. Arnold was born and raised in Ohio, but has southern roots from both of her parents. She was able to experience the presence of both grandmothers that taught her the art of storytelling. After graduating from HS, she enrolled at Alabama A&M University and obtained her degree in Marketing and later a MBA in Human Resources. However, she always remembered the stories told to her as a child. She began writing in seventh grade. Two of her poems were published during her teen years. She continued to write poems and short stories, until a friend encouraged her to finish one of her stories. This is her first published novel.

Samuel L. Dunson Jr. – Cover Illustration
Bio

Samuel L. Dunson Jr.
dunson7547@gmail.com

Education: MFA, Savannah College of Art and Design (Graduated Outstanding Painting Student, 2000), BS in Studio Art, Tennessee State University.

Samuel exhibits his paintings in group and solo shows on a regular basis. His works have been reported and critiqued in art journals and newspapers alike. Samuel teaches painting, drawing and design, as well as Art Appreciation at Tennessee State University.

Made in the USA
Charleston, SC
11 July 2016